CONVINCING THE ALPHA

HOBSON HILLS OMEGAS: BOOK EIGHT

C.W. GRAY

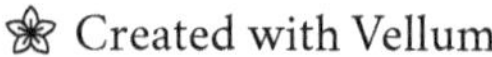 Created with Vellum

Thank you for visiting the world of Hobson Hills. I love this series and appreciate each and every one of you that read it. The events in *Convincing the Alpha* overlap with those that occurred in book seven of the Hobson Hills Omegas, *The Alpha's Christmas Wish*. While Juan and Jackson are becoming a couple, Zed and Noah are getting to know one another. Below, I've included a few family trees made by the wonderful Missy Schwarz.

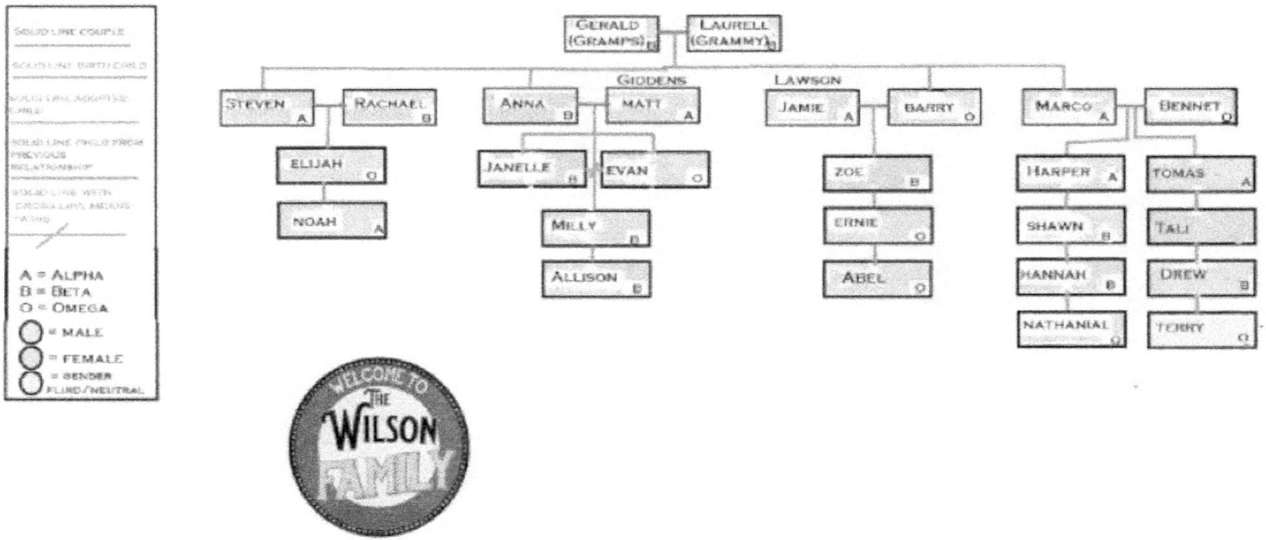

SOLID LINE COUPLE
SOLID LINE BIRTH CHILD
SOLID LINE ADOPTED CHILD
SOLID LINE CHILD FROM PREVIOUS RELATIONSHIP
SOLID LINE WITH CROSS LINE MEANS PASSED
A = ALPHA
B = BETA
O = OMEGA
= MALE
= FEMALE
= GENDER FLUID/NEUTRAL
GERALD (GRAMPS) B
LAURELL (GRAMMY) B
GIDDENS
LAWSON
STEVEN A
RACHAEL B
ANNA B
MATT A
JAMIE A
BARRY O
MARCO A
BENNET O
ELIJAH O
JANELLE B
EVAN O
ZOE B
HARPER A
TOMAS A
NOAH A
MILLY B
ERNIE O
SHAWN B
TALI A
ALLISON B
ABEL O
HANNAH B
DREW B
NATHANIAL O
TERRY O
WELCOME TO THE WILSON FAMILY

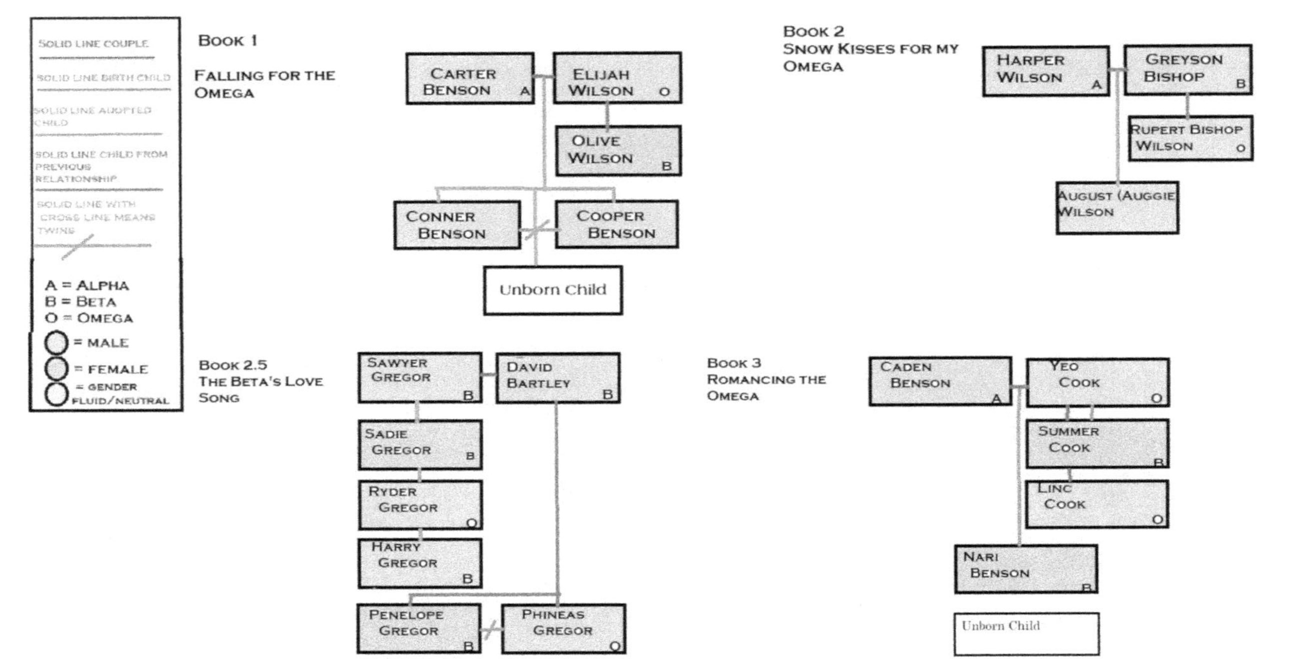

SOLID LINE COUPLE
SOLID LINE BIRTH CHILD
SOLID LINE ADOPTED CHILD
SOLID LINE CHILD FROM PREVIOUS RELATIONSHIP
SOLID LINE WITH CROSS LINE MEANS TWINS
A = ALPHA
B = BETA
O = OMEGA
= MALE
= FEMALE
= GENDER FLUID/NEUTRAL
BOOK 1
FALLING FOR THE OMEGA
CARTER BENSON A
ELIJAH WILSON O
OLIVE WILSON B
CONNER BENSON
COOPER BENSON
Unborn Child
BOOK 2.5
THE BETA'S LOVE SONG
SAWYER GREGOR B
DAVID BARTLEY B
SADIE GREGOR B
RYDER GREGOR O
HARRY GREGOR B
PENELOPE GREGOR B
PHINEAS GREGOR O
BOOK 2
SNOW KISSES FOR MY OMEGA
HARPER WILSON A
GREYSON BISHOP B
RUPERT BISHOP WILSON O
AUGUST (AUGGIE) WILSON
BOOK 3
ROMANCING THE OMEGA
CADEN BENSON A
YEO COOK O
SUMMER COOK B
LINC COOK O
NARI BENSON B
Unborn Child

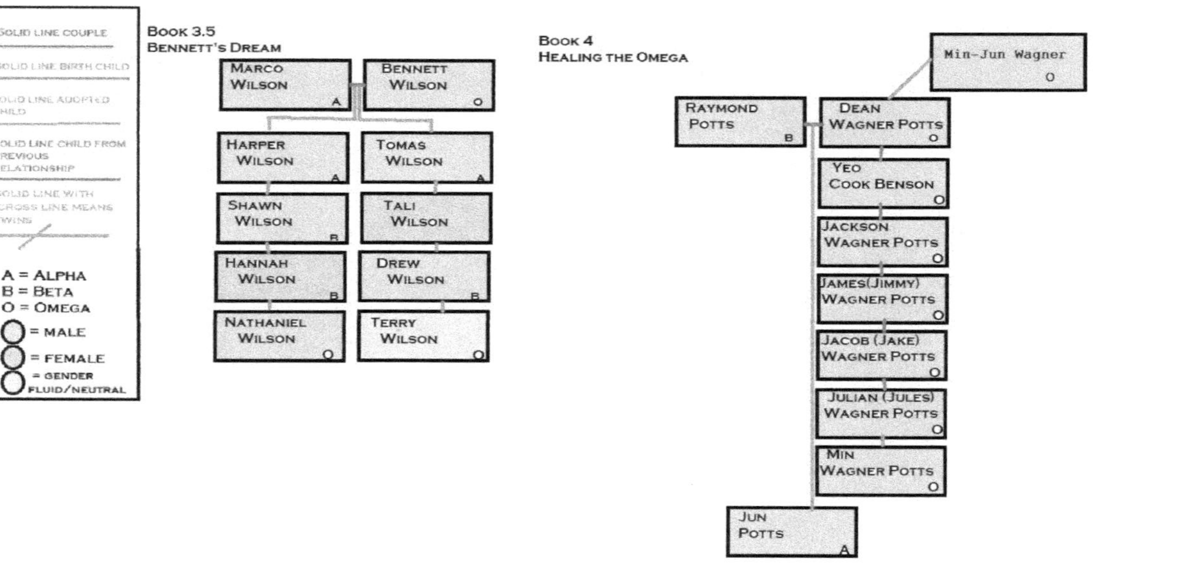

SOLID LINE COUPLE
SOLID LINE BIRTH CHILD
SOLID LINE ADOPTED CHILD
SOLID LINE CHILD FROM PREVIOUS RELATIONSHIP
SOLID LINE WITH CROSS LINE MEANS TWINS
A = ALPHA
B = BETA
O = OMEGA
= MALE
= FEMALE
= GENDER FLUID/NEUTRAL
BOOK 3.5
BENNETT'S DREAM
MARCO WILSON A
BENNETT WILSON O
HARPER WILSON A
TOMAS WILSON A
SHAWN WILSON B
TALI WILSON
HANNAH WILSON B
DREW WILSON B
NATHANIEL WILSON O
TERRY WILSON O
BOOK 4
HEALING THE OMEGA
Min-Jun Wagner O
RAYMOND POTTS B
DEAN WAGNER POTTS O
YEO COOK BENSON O
JACKSON WAGNER POTTS O
JAMES(JIMMY) WAGNER POTTS O
JACOB (JAKE) WAGNER POTTS O
JULIAN (JULES) WAGNER POTTS O
MIN WAGNER POTTS O
JUN POTTS A

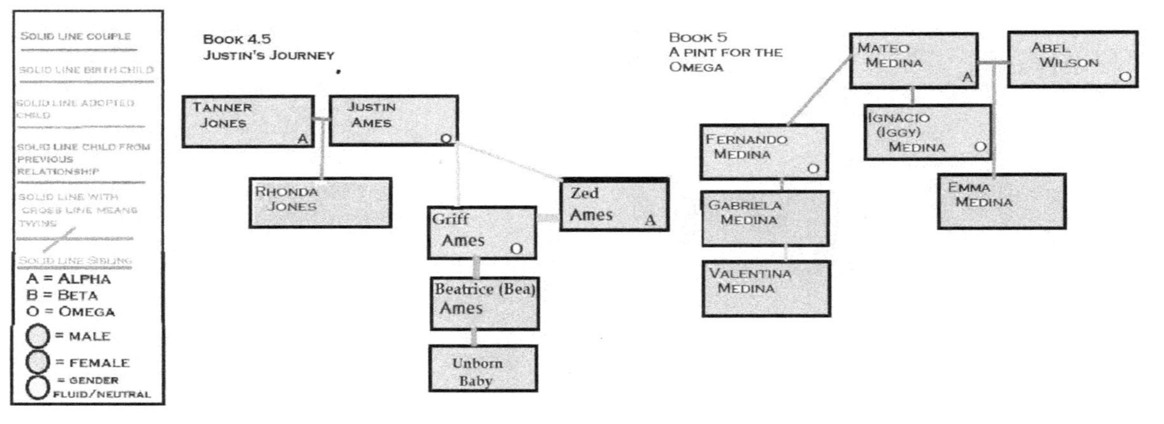

SOLID LINE COUPLE
SOLID LINE BIRTH CHILD
SOLID LINE ADOPTED CHILD
SOLID LINE CHILD FROM PREVIOUS RELATIONSHIP
SOLID LINE WITH CROSS LINE MEANS TWINS
SOLID LINE SIBLING
A = ALPHA
B = BETA
O = OMEGA
= MALE
= FEMALE
= GENDER FLUID/NEUTRAL
BOOK 4.5
JUSTIN'S JOURNEY
TANNER JONES   A
JUSTIN AMES   O
RHONDA JONES
GRIFF AMES   O
ZED AMES   A
BEATRICE (BEA) AMES
UNBORN BABY
BOOK 5
A PINT FOR THE OMEGA
MATEO MEDINA   A
ABEL WILSON   O
FERNANDO MEDINA   O
IGNACIO (IGGY) MEDINA   O
GABRIELA MEDINA
EMMA MEDINA
VALENTINA MEDINA

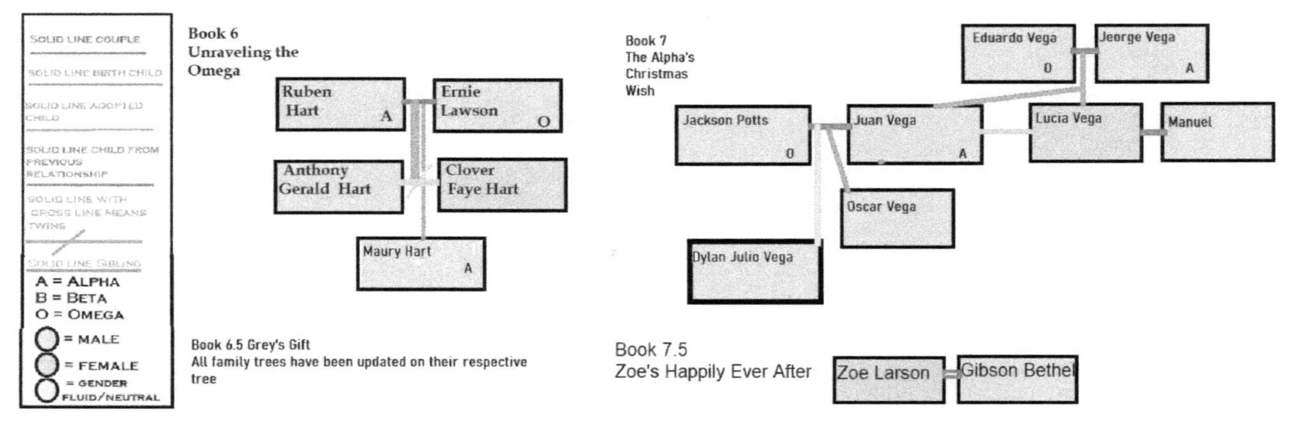

SOLID LINE COUPLE
SOLID LINE BIRTH CHILD
SOLID LINE ADOPTED CHILD
SOLID LINE CHILD FROM PREVIOUS RELATIONSHIP
SOLID LINE WITH CROSS LINE MEANS TWINS
SOLID LINE SIBLING
A = ALPHA
B = BETA
O = OMEGA
= MALE
= FEMALE
= GENDER FLUID/NEUTRAL
Book 6
Unraveling the Omega
Ruben Hart
A
Ernie Lawson
O
Anthony Gerald Hart
Clover Faye Hart
Maury Hart
A
Book 6.5 Grey's Gift
All family trees have been updated on their respective tree
Book 7
The Alpha's Christmas Wish
Eduardo Vega
O
Jeorge Vega
A
Jackson Potts
O
Juan Vega
A
Lucia Vega
Manuel
Oscar Vega
Dylan Julio Vega
Book 7.5
Zoe's Happily Ever After
Zoe Larson
Gibson Bethel

CHAPTER 1

OCTOBER

*N*oah Wilson perched precariously on a ladder and gently placed an apple into his basket before reaching for another. Since he had a little trouble with balance, it had taken some arguing to get assigned a ladder position, but Noah could be as stubborn as any other Wilson, and they had a lot of work to do.

Noah took a moment to breath the sweet scent of apples and cool fall air. The apple trees in Elijah's orchard were heavy with fruit, and the whole Wilson family gathered to help Noah's brother with the last harvest of the season.

Elijah danced below as he picked the apples hanging on the lower branches of Noah's tree. His lips moved as he sang, and Noah smiled and wished he could hear Elijah sing. Then again, with how often Olive complained about him being off-key, maybe Noah should be happy he couldn't hear him.

Elijah caught his smile and winked at him. "Do you need a break? I can work from the ladder."

It took a moment for Noah to process his brother's words. He speechread well, but it took time, more time than some people were willing to spend on him for a simple conversation.

"No." Noah shook his head and went back to work. Ever since Noah moved to Hobson Hills, Elijah had embraced being an overprotective big brother. If Noah so much as sneezed, Elijah pulled out the allergy medicine and thermometer.

His ladder shook a little, and he looked down.

Elijah held up a bottle of water. "Hydrate." The stubborn look on his face told Noah he had best just accept the coddling.

At least he isn't making me get off the ladder. Noah smiled wryly and took the water. "I'm okay, Eli. It's not even hot."

Elijah hugged his leg, then went back to dancing and picking apples.

Elijah's husband, Carter, started to pass them with a basket of apples but stopped when he saw Elijah dancing. His eyes heated, and a familiar expression covered his face. Carter set his basket down.

"No, don't do it." Noah wrinkled his nose, well aware of what that expression meant. Unfortunately. "If you two start, you'll never stop."

Carter spun Elijah around and bent him over his arm for a kiss.

"And… there goes our productivity." Noah's shoulders slumped when the two's kiss got a little out of control. They were at the bottom of his ladder, so he couldn't move on to the next tree. He looked around for help, but everyone looked busy.

Noah sighed and took one more drink of water before he dumped the rest over their heads.

Carter jumped back and glared at him, making Noah smile.

Elijah slapped Noah's leg and said something, lips moved too fast for him to read.

He grinned. Elijah was probably cursing.

Carter picked up his basket and walked away, nose in the air.

Elijah propped his hands on his hips and pouted. "That was mean." His lips moved at a normal rate this time.

"I'm not sorry." The slight strain on his throat told him he had likely said that too loudly. *Oops.*

He climbed off the ladder and combined his basket with Elijah's, then ruffled Elijah's hair, making his brother scowl. "I envy you two."

Elijah's eyes widened, and his mouth formed a little round *O* of surprise. "Really? You want an omega of your own? Are you saying you're ready to start dating?"

After processing Elijah's words, Noah shrugged. "I don't know. I'm not unhappy exactly. I love my job and being close to the family. It's just that sometimes I want a little more. I think I might be ready to try to get out there. Maybe."

Noah may not have been able to hear Elijah's squeal, but he knew the whole orchard had to have noticed it. Elijah shook his arms over his head and hopped around, flailing like he was being attacked by bees.

Elijah really can't dance, he thought for probably the thousandth time in his life. Noah couldn't catch even half of what his brother was saying, but he recognized one word. *Zoe.*

"No, no, no." He grabbed Elijah's shoulders and pulled his brother to him, muffling Elijah's words with his hand. He looked around to see how much attention they had garnered. "Damn it."

Zoe smiled widely and ran to them, fingers dancing quickly as she signed. "Noah, I know so many omegas to match you with. We'll start this weekend."

"No, thank you." He shook his head. "I'm perfectly capable of… Holy shit!"

Grammy and Aunt Anna ambushed him with a hug from behind, and he stumbled before righting himself.

Anna practically glowed when she leaned back. "Donnie Milligun has an omega nephew your age," she said, carefully enunciating. "I call dibs on the weekend after next."

Grammy kissed his cheek. "You'll be a good father, Noah. You already spend so much time with Olive and the twins."

Maybe they aren't saying what I think they're saying. He whimpered and looked around for help.

Uncle Marco gave him a sympathetic look and pulled him away from the growing horde of Wilsons. "Back to work, Wilsons. We have apples to harvest." Marco hugged him. "Leave Noah alone."

Elijah smirked. "If you insist, Uncle Marco."

Noah stayed close to Marco for the rest of the morning. His uncle was one of his favorite people. Marco was a quiet man with a comfortable presence. Noah didn't have to work hard to understand him or struggle to express himself. With his uncle, he could just be. When they spoke, it was usually through American Sign Language, which made it intensely easier for Noah to really participate in the conversation.

While Noah was very good at speechreading and used that to communicate most of the time, the majority of his family and friends had learned Signed English when Noah came to live in Hobson Hills. It took some of the load of communicating off Noah's shoulders when he was stressed or confused.

A few, however, had joined him in learning ASL as well. Noah had been surprised at how much he preferred the more complex language. It had taken him time, and he still had so much to learn, but ASL was quicker and more expressive to use than Signed English or speechreading. He didn't have to guess at what people meant. They just told him.

When he lost his hearing, he hadn't known a thing about sign language, little less that there were so many types or that ASL was a whole language all on its own. It had been a very confusing time in more ways than one. Noah shivered and pushed his thoughts away, wanting to enjoy the rest of the day.

They moved from tree to tree until the last of the apples were loaded in the back of Gramps's truck. They would sell some of the apples in their family's store,

Farm Fresh, but Elijah would use the majority of them to make apple bread, apple cider, apple wine, and a thousand other apple products.

I need to remember to grab a loaf of apple bread before I go home today, Noah thought. His stomach growled, and he smiled as he felt the vibration under his hand. He looked around for Grammy. She and Grey were always in charge of the food.

He spotted them beneath a few of the larger apple trees. Grey smiled softly, eyes full of contentment as he spread another blanket on the ground. He loved taking care of other people, especially by feeding them. Grammy was the same. She smiled brightly and practically wiggled in place as she set out the food.

Elijah gets his love of dancing from her, Noah thought, smiling. Sometimes he let himself envy Elijah's close relationships with the rest of the family. Noah's brother had grown up with Grammy and Gramps and all the other Wilsons. Noah had grown up with their asshole parents.

Marco gripped his shoulder, drawing his attention. His fingers moved deftly as he signed, "I'm happy that you're ready to start dating again. I know you wanted to adjust to your hearing loss, but it's been a while. Bennett and I were worried that you would cut yourself off from the world."

Noah breathed out slowly and tried to keep his voice low. "It's easier to be alone."

Marco gave him an understanding look. "Yes, but it's damn lonely."

And lonely gets old after a while. Noah looked around

the orchard. Even when he was surrounded by friends and family, he still felt alone sometimes.

Elijah pushed between them and linked arms with Noah. "I'm hungry."

Noah kissed the top of his omega brother's head. "Me too."

Arms wrapped around his waist, and Noah smiled softly. Olive squeezed him once, then let him go. She signed, "I love you," then ran to catch up with the other younger Wilsons.

Noah looked at Elijah. "I think you should give me Olive since I don't have any kids and you have three."

Elijah shook with laughter. "She's the best behaved. Take one of the others."

"Not until they're potty trained." Noah grabbed Marco's arm with his free hand. "I should get Elijah's piece of cherry pie, right, Uncle Marco? Since he won't give me Olive."

Marco threw his head back, laughing. Noah didn't catch his answer, but he knew his uncle. Marco would give Noah his pie.

THE BED SHAKER UNDER HIS PILLOW VIBRATED, AND THE motion pulled Noah from sleep. His heart beat fast as he reached out, hands shaking, to turn the alarm off. He should feel well-rested after a full night's sleep, but Noah was exhausted. *Stupid dreams*, he thought.

He yawned and rolled out of bed, standing still for a moment to center himself. The openness of the high ceilings in his room helped him breath, and the tension in his neck started to ease. In his dream, he'd been tied down to the hospital bed in the tiny room of the institution. It was a familiar dream.

He shook his body and released a big breath. *Enough of that. We have a big day today.*

No one was here to look at him strangely, so he stomped his feet a few times, smiling at the vibrations. Sometimes he wondered if other deaf people got a thrill from things like this too. *Not asking Diane that question,* he thought and snorted. His friend was a CODA, a child of deaf adults, and had been a huge help to him in adjusting to losing his hearing, but he still held back asking her about things that embarrassed him. *Maybe one day.*

After working through his morning routine, he dressed in jeans and a sweater, then made his way downstairs for his coffee. He could already smell it brewing, the rich scent sending a shiver down his back.

Elijah and his family had gotten the fancy coffee machine for Noah's birthday, and he'd never loved a gift more. It had a timer, and he could make everything from an expresso to a plain black cup of coffee.

Elijah gives me too much, he thought fondly. When his brother saved Noah and brought him to Hobson Hills, he'd given Noah an old water mill to renovate into a home.

Noah was proud of his place. It had plenty of space, high ceilings with wooden beams, and refurbished stone walls. The water wheel even still worked. It converted water flow into energy for Noah's home. It didn't power everything, but it made his utilities a bit cheaper.

Elijah gave me a life. Noah swallowed the lump in his throat. He hated dreaming about the institution. It did things to his head and made him maudlin.

Rain fell against the windows of the living room, and he stopped a moment to look out into the dark. He remembered the sound of rain falling and tried to line the memory with the raindrops, but it didn't quite work. Now it was just silence.

He pressed his hand to the glass and tapped his fingers against the smooth, cool window pane. It was still mostly dark out, but he could see glints of light on Wright Mill Creek. They were getting plenty of rain this fall, so the current was fast and the creek overfull. He thought of the rush of water and the sound it would make.

Enough of that. Noah yawned again and followed his nose to his coffee. He pulled out his favorite mug, a gift from Olive, and smiled. It had a horse silhouette with a lightsaber and said *May the horse be with you.*

He sipped his coffee and took his time making breakfast. This was his favorite time of day. Most of the world was still asleep and everything was *quiet.* Completely losing his hearing had made everything silent, but there was more than one way for the world to be *loud.*

A flash of his dream made him drop his spatula. He shuddered at the memory of the orderlies shaking him and slapping his face to get his attention. He felt some noise escape him. He had tried so hard to read the words on their lips, but his mind had been fogged from the drugs the doctors had pumped into him and his hearing loss had been so new. All he had been able to do was scream until his throat gave out.

Noah evened his breathing again and got a new spatula. He scooped the bacon from the frying pan to his plate before starting on the eggs. His time in the fucking institution haunted him more than the violent attack that had caused him to lose his hearing.

Diane told him it was the loss of control he'd suffered there. Sometimes he wished his therapist wasn't so damn insightful.

It's going to be a good day, he told himself. *Saul and Emmet are coming by, Diane's bringing a new patient, and Dean works today.*

By his second cup of coffee, his dreams were locked away, and he was ready to start the day.

He sat at the kitchen table and watched the sun rise through the windows. It really was his favorite time of the day. There was no struggling to understand anyone, no trying to piece together the conversation around him. Just peace.

He felt his phone buzz in his pocket and looked at the text.

Olive: Love you, Uncle Noah!

Noah smiled. Every single morning his niece texted him. He sent back a message wishing her luck on the presentation she was giving in school today and his phone buzzed again.

Ray: Dean's bringing lunch for everyone today. I found honey ham on sale yesterday.

Noah shook his head. Ray had turned into a big mama bear since marrying Dean. He replied back and had just pushed send when it buzzed again.

Juan: Poker night this week will be a hunt instead. Ernie and I want to check out the woods by The Irish Rose. Be there with all your gear, little alpha.

Noah groaned. Damn it, he hated those damn Big Foot excursions. *Ernie and Juan enjoy them, though.* He put his phone up. *Fucking Bigfoot.*

He checked the clock on the wall. If he didn't get moving, he'd be running late.

He thought about his uncle's words from the day before. Loneliness was something that was only now really pulling at him. Right after Elijah rescued him, Noah's life had been about adjusting to a new normal. He hadn't had time to be lonely. In fact, he had needed time alone to recover from the exhaustion that came with constantly struggling to communicate with a hearing world.

Now, sometimes when he was by himself, it actually felt *lonely.* Of course, his family still didn't leave him alone often. *Maybe it wouldn't be so bad sharing my mornings.*

He put his dishes in the dishwasher and pulled on his boots. He didn't bother locking the door to the house. His horse ranch was literally in his backyard.

The chill of the air tickled his nose as he walked across the wooden bridge leading from his back porch to the other side of the creek. Water rushed below and he stopped a moment to admire his water wheel. Watching it turn fascinated him for some reason.

A new fern caught his eye. The bushy green plant sat between two swamp azaleas in the flowerbed next to his porch. "Janelle," he muttered. Every time he turned around, Janelle had somehow managed to plant something else in the shaded flowerbed.

He shook his head and hurried across the bridge. He had two large barns on the five acres directly behind his house. One barn was meant for rescued horses that needed a little time to adjust to people, and the other was for his therapy horses.

The familiar smell of horse, hay, and dirt greeted him as he entered the rescue barn and made him smile. For the past three years, Noah had immersed himself in all things horse and had managed to find a place for himself and the animals he loved so much.

Seven horses watched him with dark, liquid eyes. Currently, he had three rescues that needed major attention and four that just needed to finish adapting to their new home. They all wanted their breakfast though.

The three in the back had special diets, so he put together their breakfasts and refreshed their hay. Jake, Dean's son, would be by after school to muck all the stalls. Horse shit was one thing that Noah *didn't* necessarily like about horses, not that he didn't do his own amount of shoveling.

He emptied the last can of grain mixture into Carrot's feed dish, then turned to go. The Paint horse grabbed the back of Noah's shirt and shook his head, stopping Noah from moving away.

Carrot slowly tugged him back, and Noah grinned,

turning to rub Carrot's soft and bristly nose. The gelding had only arrived a few days ago, but Noah already loved him. He was malnourished and dehydrated from the neglect of his previous owner, but somehow the horse's big personality had survived the abuse.

Noah stroked Carrot's neck and tried for soft, soothing noises. It must have worked because Carrot pushed his head against Noah's chest. Noah pressed his face to the horse's neck and breathed in his earthy horse smell.

He knew there were others he needed to care for, but it was hard to leave Carrot behind.

"You need rest, buddy." Noah leaned back and rubbed Carrot's forehead. "The farrier is coming today, and he'll take a look at your hoofs. If he gives the go ahead, I'll take you with me on rounds tomorrow. Okay?"

Carrot grabbed his shirt and pulled him closer again.

Noah laughed and grabbed the brush hanging on the stall wall. "I guess, I have time for pampering."

He lost track of time as he brushed Carrot's pretty brown and white coat. His mane and tail were both a mix of brown and white hair, and Noah knew Carrot would be gorgeous once he was back to his full health.

The flickering lights in the barn caught his attention, and he looked over his shoulder. Dean leaned against the wall. The older omega smiled softly as he watched Noah.

Noah flushed and patted Carrot's flank. "Sorry. I got distracted."

"Carrot is attached to you," Dean said. "It's sweet."

Noah rubbed Carrot's nose one more time, then forced himself to leave his stall. "I'm attached to him too, but we have a lot of horses to feed, and I just took care of these three."

Dean shrugged. "I'm here now." He bumped Noah with his shoulder. "I heard you'll be married with five kids before the end of the year."

Noah snorted. "If Elijah, Grammy, and Aunt Anna have their way, I will be."

"Well, I'm here if you need to talk." Dean wrinkled his nose, eyes briefly flashing with sadness. "Not that I'm any good at dating. I never had the chance before I met Ray."

"How's this pickup line?" Noah wiggled his brows, hoping to make Dean laugh. "Did you fart? Because you just blew me away."

Dean stared at him in horror until Noah started laughing. "Damn it, Noah. For a moment, I thought you were serious."

CHAPTER 2

Zed Ames watered his fern, then fluffed its long, bushy fronds. "You have a good day, pretty girl. When I get home, I'll tell you all about my day."

His phone buzzed in his pocket, and he read the text from Griff.

Griff: You're coming to lunch today, right? Justin and I have a surprise for you.

Zed rolled his eyes. He fluffed his fern's fronds again. "I love my brothers, Eugenia. I swear I do, but they're annoying. How much do you want to bet they try to set me up with an omega today?"

Eugenia's elegant fronds fell back into place, and Zed swore she smiled at him.

"You're right. A surprise date isn't quite their style." He rubbed chin. "They're up to something though."

His phone buzzed.

Griff: Zed? You're coming, right?

Zed: Yeah, I'll be there. Going to work now.

Zed tucked his phone back in his pocket and blew Eugenia a kiss. "Have a good day."

He grabbed his thermos of coffee and locked the door behind him. The house Abel had set Zed up with was nice. The former owners had used it as a vacation house, but they had taken good care of it.

The two-story cabin was nestled in a wooded clearing and was only a couple of miles from the hops farm and brewery where Zed worked. The house came with the job and had made moving here after he left the Marines a lot easier.

He found the path he had made last week, then quickly jogged through the woods to the brewery. The fall air was crisp and a little cold this early in the morning, but Zed enjoyed the exercise.

He passed one of their newest hops fields before he reached brewery. Zed had missed the summer harvest since he had only arrived in Hobson Hills a couple of weeks ago, but he had already helped Janelle prep the hops fields for next year and started learning about the brewing process from Abel.

He jogged in place for a moment outside the brewery and unlocked the door. Abel wouldn't be in for a couple of hours, so Zed set his thermos down at his work table and checked the schedule. They had two different sets of beer to start today.

He readied the grist in the masher and started the machine. While he waited for the masher to finish, he swept the floors and quickly dusted the machinery. Zed was already attached to the place and wanted it to look its best.

Abel's brewery was small, but Zed had still been amazed when he'd learned Abel had done most of the work himself until recently. It was a lot of work for two people, little less one, but Abel was a hard worker and didn't shirk his responsibilities when things got tough. Zed liked that.

Now, he had Zed to help. *Not that I'm that much help,* he thought wryly. He was learning the ropes, but brewing was a completely new process to him. He liked it so far. He had a lot of time to himself, and Abel was a good boss. He showed Zed how to do something, watched him a couple of times, then left him to it. There was no looking over his shoulder the whole day or criticizing the way he did things.

He washed his hands and moved the malted barley to the boiling water in the brewing kettle. Afterward, he watched the temperature carefully. He didn't want to ruin the malt.

Zed looked up when the door opened.

Janelle held up a potted English ivy plant. "I brought Eugenia a little sister. Her name is Maude."

He grinned. Most folks thought he was crazy for naming and talking to a plant, but Janelle got him. The woman was quickly becoming his favorite person, aside from his niece of course.

"She'll be jealous at first, but I think she'll adapt to a sibling." He scowled. "I did."

Janelle chuckled. "Are Griff and Justin annoying you again?"

"Yeah, they keep talking about setting me up with omegas they know." Zed lowered the temperature on the kettle. Now, he could relax and let the machine do its thing. "I'm not eager to jump into a relationship yet. I'm still getting used to being a civilian, and I just want to focus on settling in, you know?"

Janelle handed him Maude. "I get it. I think they want you hooked up with someone so you'll stay around."

Zed gave her a surprised look. "I'm not going anywhere."

She shrugged. "Think about it. As soon as you could, you enlisted and left Griff. At least, that's how he sees it, and while you were a Marine, you weren't around often. Now you're back, and maybe he wants something tying you to Hobson Hills."

Zed grunted. Maybe she was right. Sometimes he wished he hadn't left Griff so quickly. Zed had needed a job, and the Marine Corps fit him well.

"Then there's Justin. He's still getting used to having you at all, and he's happily married now." She scowled. "Happily married people are all about spreading the love."

He snorted. "You're speaking from experience, huh?"

She made a face. "Unfortunately."

Zed set Maude down on a work table. "I don't know if you're right. Griff, Justin, and Bea are here. That's all it takes to keep me in Hobson Hills. I did my duty, now I'm ready to start my life."

"They'll figure that out." Janelle hopped up on the worktable. "Now, let's go over my plans for the new fields behind your house. We need to get them ready if we're going to plant them in the spring."

Zed sat on the table beside her. "Yes, ma'am."

ZED PARKED HIS TRUCK OUTSIDE THE IRISH ROSE. THE place was packed, but there was some benefit to being related to one of the owners. Justin and Griff were already seated at a table on the patio.

The air was a little cool, but still comfortable. The patio section of the pub overlooked a thick wooded area. The trees were quickly losing their leaves, but the remaining red, gold, and orange foliage was a pretty sight.

Bea held her arms out for him as soon as she saw him.

Zed grabbed his niece and swung her in the air, smiling at her giggles. "Are you ready for lunch, honey bee?"

Bea hugged him and nodded. "Need yum yums."

He settled her back into her highchair. "Let's get my girl some yum yums."

Justin watched him with a soft look in his eyes. "You need kids, Zed."

Zed groaned. "This again? I'm a good uncle. I have my honey bee and soon we'll have little Ronnie too." He bent and kissed the top of Justin's head. "Can I?"

Griff snickered at Justin's scowl. "You know he has to do it, Jus."

Justin pushed his chair back and sighed. "Go ahead."

Zed leaned down and kissed Justin's very large pregnant belly. His younger brother was due within the next week, and he looked like he'd give birth any moment. "Hi, baby Ronnie. Uncle Zed loves you and can't wait to meet you."

Griff snapped a picture. "That is so dang cute."

Zed chuckled and sat down, reaching for a menu. "I know I'm adorable. Where's Tanner?"

"He picked up an extra shift. He's trying to get in as many hours as he can before the baby comes." Justin sipped his tea. "By the way, we already ordered."

Zed grunted and put the menu back down. "What did you order me?"

"What you always get," Griff said, rolling his eyes at Justin.

"Reuben sandwich, a dill pickle, and side salad," Griff and Justin said at the same time.

"Are you saying I'm predictable?" Zed asked and tugged on Bea's foot, making his niece laugh again.

Griff propped his chin on his fist. "Very predictable. Now, are you ready for your surprise?"

"Do I have a choice?" he asked, brow raised.

"Nope." Justin grinned. "Friday night you have a date with an omega named Sam. He works with Rueben in the kitchen and just moved to Hobson Hills."

Griff waved his hands in the air. "Yay!"

"No." Zed looked at the picture Bea was coloring. "Is that a horse?"

"Horsey pretty." Bea pursed her lips. "Kiss me."

Zed obeyed his niece and gave her a kiss.

"What do mean, *no*?" Griff pushed a glass of water

in front of Zed. "Sam is a nice guy, and you need to get out and have some fun."

Zed sipped his water. "Sam and I have met, and he is a nice guy. By the way, I have fun all the time."

Griff leaned back, overacting his shock. "What's this? You have fun doing what exactly?"

"I like working on the hops farm." He shrugged. "It's fun."

"Abel told me you've been putting in twelve-hour days." Justin narrowed his eyes. "How many hours did you sleep last night?"

Zed ignored him and helped Bea color her horse.

"I think the better question are how many hours did you spend exercising and how many times did you clean the house last night." Griff's voice was soft with concern. "Zed, we're worried about you. You clean your house like you're expecting an inspection, and you actually made sandbags to do those lifty exercises as if you were still enlisted."

"Cleaning and exercising aren't bad habits." He thought about what Janelle said. "I'm not going to run off like Dad."

Griff looked shocked. "I never thought you would. You're my steady rock, Zed. I know you're nothing like Dad."

Joshua Ames had kept two families at the same time, each unaware of the other. Zed was sad *and* happy that his mom never knew about that. She had been torn up enough when Joshua had abandoned them. Zed and Griff had only found out recently when they met their half-brother, Justin.

Justin gave him a concerned look. "You are definitely not like *him*. We're worried because you only go to thc brewery, then home. Nowhere else."

"I meet you two for lunch almost every day." Zed focused on coloring and made sure the horse's leg was a perfectly even brown. "Janelle and I even went to her cousin Harper's house and planted a row of black cherry trees near his barn. Granted she insisted we sneak and do it in the middle of the night, but still."

Bea giggled and colored over his masterpiece with a red crayon before leaning over and kissing his cheek.

Zed stuck his tongue out, then went back to coloring.

"Zed, we want you to be happy here." Justin bit his lip. "I can't imagine it's easy to adjust to being a civilian, but maybe if you went out more, you'd make friends that didn't lure you into trespassing to plant trees."

"Janelle's great." Zed ignored the red lines and colored the horse's hoof black. "I kind of like Tanner too."

Justin snorted. "Well, that's a relief since he's my husband and all."

Their server, an alpha named North, set their food in front of them.

Zed narrowed his eyes on the man. North watched Griff like he was the last cookie on the plate. For his brother's part, he seemed oblivious.

"Thanks, North," Justin said, smiling at the man. "Is it busy inside?"

North nodded quickly. "We're really getting pounded in the back."

Griff raised a brow. "You're getting pounded in the back, huh? TMI, man."

Justin smacked Griff's arm. "Leave him alone, Griff. Thanks, North. We appreciate the food."

"No problem." North licked his lips. "You look like you're about to have that baby any minute, boss. I guess the salad you ordered was a good choice."

Justin gave North an amazed look and shook his head. "Oh, North. I know that probably sounded different in your head."

Griff growled. "Did you just call my brother fat? Do you know how hard it is to maintain a healthy weight while you're pregnant? His hormones are all out of whack and he's not getting enough rest. He doesn't need some jerk wad telling him he's fat."

"I'll just go now." North spun around and ran for the door.

Justin laughed. "I swear, Griff, if you're around, North says the worst thing possible. When you're not here, he's a sweetheart."

"Whatever." Griff pointed a fry at Zed. "You'll meet Sam here at six on Friday night. The date has been made, and you'll honor it."

Zed grumbled but nodded. He didn't want to date anyone, but he also didn't want to stand the omega up. Sam really was a nice guy.

An hour later, he left the pub and headed back to his truck. Someone with a horse trailer took up two spaces beside him, and he couldn't resist looking in the trailer.

A curious brown nose booped his chin. The

miniature horse in the first stall nuzzled at his hand when he reached down to pet her. She had a spotted brown and white butt and a more solid brown and white body. Two other miniatures were in the trailer. One was black and white, and the other was a rich dark brown.

The girl closest to him whinnied, drawing his attention. He patted her nose and carefully ran his hand through her brown and white mane.

"Hey, you." He laughed when she slobbered all over his hand. "I don't have any treats, beautiful."

"I gave them plenty of treats before I went in to lunch," a man said from behind him.

Zed turned around quickly and rubbed the horse's slobber on his jeans. "Sorry. I couldn't resist petting her."

The old man's smile was kind. "Meet Peanut, Butter, and Jelly."

Zed laughed. "Those are really their names?"

The man laughed. "Yep. Their owner was a dear friend of mine. She just moved to a retirement home in Florida, and I promised to find them a good home." He held his hand out. "I'm Duncan Grover. I run the veterinarian office here in Hobson Hills."

Zed shook the man's hand with his clean one. "Zed Ames."

Grover's eyes lit up. "You're Justin's brother. He told me to keep an eye out for a dog or cat for you."

Zed held his hands up. "Whoa there. I don't need a pet." He smiled at the three horses and went back to petting them. "These three will make someone happy.

They're hard to resist. If I had a barn, I might… Oh, never mind." He laughed when Peanut slobbered all over his hand again.

Grover rubbed his chin. "Hmm, you know you could stable them until you built a barn. Peanut likes you awful well, and Jelly and Butter always follow her lead."

Zed shook his head. "I really shouldn't."

Grover's smile was strained. "I'm just worried about keeping them together. They were raised together and are really attached to one another. It will be hard finding them a home." He sighed. "I'll just keep them in the back field behind my office, I guess. I worry about coyotes getting to them, but what else can I do?"

Zed's eyes went to the three miniatures. Jelly, the black and white horse, nickered softly, dark brown eyes giving him a soulful look. Butter, the dark brown horse, ducked his head, looking dejected. They would be no match for a pack of coyotes.

Abel won't mind if I fence in around the house and build a small barn, Zed thought to himself. His boss was almost as bad as Justin and Griff when it came to pets, and he had been clear the house was Zed's as long as he worked at the brewery and farm.

"Let me see if I can find a place to stable them. I have a little land I can pasture them on, but it will take time to build a barn for them."

Grover smiled wide. "I know a man that has a horse therapy ranch. His name is Noah. Here, I'll get his card for you. I know he'd stable them for you. That boy is horse crazy." He handed Zed a card. "I'll drop them off for you right now. I can't wait to text Bertie and let her know her babies have a good home and won't get eaten by coyotes."

Zed clutched the card and watched as Grover jumped into his truck and drove away. "Did I just adopt three miniature horses?"

$\mathcal{N}$oah stood in Stinkbug's stall with Diane's new patient, Jared. "First, you should use a curry." He handed it to the young beta and helped him brush a small circle on Stinkbug's neck. "With this one, pretend you're washing a window and make circles all over Stink's body. Curry combs help get all the dirt out of his coat. He has a habit of rolling around in the pasture."

Jared gave him a reluctant smile and mumbled something Noah didn't catch.

Noah stifled his annoyance. He hated it when people didn't face him when they talked. *Jared is shy*, he reminded himself.

Diane signed for Jared, eyes sympathetic. "He rolls around like a dog?"

Noah snorted and patted Stinkbug's neck. "Yeah, he's a character. He also likes beer. A couple of my friends came over for a drink a few months ago, and Stinkbug actually stole a glass of beer and guzzled it."

Jared shook with laughter and pressed his face against Stinkbug's side.

Diane signed from where she leaned against the stall rail. "This is helping him. He hasn't laughed like this in all the months I've known him."

Jared leaned back, worry replacing his laughter. "Wait. Is beer okay for horses?" He spoke a little too fast, but Noah was able to figure out what he asked through context and a few recognized words.

"Yeah, in moderation." Noah started brushing Stinkbug again. "I sneak him a little beer in his water every now and then."

Jared smiled again and worked on Stinkbug's other side. "I like him."

The rest of the morning went fast. Jared learned how to feed, water, and brush Stinkbug fairly quickly. Diane would bring him to Noah's once a week until he felt comfortable either coming on his own or needed to move on to a new type of therapy.

Noah waved as they drove away. Jared and Stinkbug were a good fit. The horse was a rescue and both gentle and playful. He'd help the omega find a little peace from whatever was haunting him.

He joined Dean, Emmet, and Saul for sandwiches in the breakroom. Ray made the best sandwiches, and Noah didn't know how he did it. When Noah made his own, it just tasted like a sandwich, but if Ray made it, somehow the sandwich tasted ten times better.

Dean held out a plate of food for him after he washed his hands. "I watched you and Jared a little. Stinkbug's the one for him."

"I think so too." Noah yawned, then bit into his sandwich.

Saul scowled. "Stinkbug."

"Your mortal enemy," Noah said between bites. "The thief that stole your beer."

Emmet chuckled and bumped Saul with his shoulder. "How can you not like Stinkbug?"

Noah lost track of the conversation and focused on his food when the two started picking on one another. Saul and Emmet had both started out as patients of Diane's. Eventually, they'd become good friends and came to the ranch often to visit with Noah and the horses.

Noah wished they were there all the time. They were good company even if Dean's teenage son was more mature than them.

Dean rolled his eyes at the two men, and Noah smiled, leaning over to whisper in the omega's ear. "Do you have a Band-Aid? I scraped my knee when I fell for you."

He must not have been too successful with the whispering because Emmet gave him a shocked look, while a flash of anger stole across Saul's face before he managed to hide it behind a cold look.

Dean covered his face and shook with laughter. He looked up after a moment. "You're terrible. Where do you even find these pickup lines?"

"What the fuck, Noah?" Emmet crossed his arms. "Are you trying something with Ray's husband? That's just wrong, man."

Noah arched a brow. "Does that sound like

something I would do?"

"No," Saul said, slowly, relief replacing the frozen anger. "What's going on here?"

Dean smirked. "Noah has a date this weekend. Everyone is setting him up with their omega friends and family."

Emmet grinned. "I know an omega that would be perfect for you."

Noah groaned. "Not you too. Just leave me alone. All I did was mention that I might be open to dating again, and everyone suddenly has the perfect omega for me."

The other three turned to the door, so Noah turned around.

Doc Grover smiled as he walked in. He made sure he faced Noah and spoke as clearly as possible, but Noah still had to guess a bit on what he was saying. "I've got three miniatures I need you to stable for a man."

Noah's eyes widened. "Three miniature horses?"

Doc nodded. "Justin and Griff's brother is adopting them."

"Zed?" Noah asked.

Doc nodded again.

Noah hadn't met Justin and Griff's brother yet, but it wouldn't be long before the Wilsons descended on the man. He was new to town and working for Noah's cousin, so it was almost certain he'd be pulled into the Wilson circle.

He frowned. "Wait. Why is he adopting horses if he doesn't have somewhere to put them?"

Doc gave him a smug look. "Justin wanted Zed to have a pet."

Noah rolled his eyes. "You conned him into three miniatures."

Doc grinned smugly. "He's easier than Carter."

Dean shook his head. "I'll help you unload them."

Noah grabbed his hat. "I guess I'll get some stalls ready. Poor guy doesn't know what's in store for him."

LATER THAT AFTERNOON, AFTER EMMET AND SAUL HAD left, Noah checked over the three miniatures. He fastened a hair clip in Peanut's soft, wiry mane. "You're the queen of the pack, aren't you?"

The pintaloosa gave him a sweet look and munched on her hay.

He moved on to Butter. The brown dun was a little rounder than he should be, and Noah made a mental note to exercise him a bit. Their previous owner hadn't been able to do much with them because of her health. They were well-fed and clearly well-loved, but all three were energetic and eager to play.

Noah took his straw cowboy hat off and put it on Butter's head. The horse bumped him with his soft nose, then went back to his feed.

"Miss Jelly, how about another hairclip? Olive leaves them at the house all the time." Noah stroked the black and white pinto's neck and smoothed out her mane before fastening the red butterfly clip.

Dean's son Jake set his shovel down and leaned over

the gate. "I need to steal some of Nari's hair clips for Jelly. I think she's my favorite."

Noah grinned. "Don't let Peanut know. She's the queen, you know."

Peanut tossed her head and gave Jake a baleful look, her lips shaking as she nickered.

Jake gave him a wide-eyed amused look, then collapsed against the fence laughing.

Noah laughed with him, shaking his head. *Miss Priss really is the queen.*

After a few moments, Jake bumped him with his shoulder. "I'm going to help Papa clean the stalls in the other barn. I'm here this weekend, right?"

"Are you sure you're alright working every weekend? You need to make sure you have time for homework."

Jake rolled his eyes. "Dad doesn't let me forget the homework."

Noah patted his shoulder. "Okay then. See you Saturday."

Jake grabbed his shovel and ran for the door. The kid was way too energetic and happy about shoveling shit. Noah liked him a lot. Jake loved horses as much as Noah and Dean, and he was a hard worker.

His phone vibrated in his back pocket, and he pulled it out, still smiling.

His smile disappeared when he read the text. *This is your father. I need money and I need it now. You owe me, Noah. I went to PRISON because of you and that bitch omega brother of yours. I'll text you my account number. Don't disappoint me.*

The phone tumbled from Noah's trembling hand, and he slid down Jelly's stall door. *No, no, no. He's in prison, and he can't come near me.* His body shook uncontrollably, and he closed his eyes. *He's in prison, and he can't come near me.*

A large, calloused hand took Noah's own, startling him. His looked up into a pair of warm brown eyes. The man kneeling in front of him was in his late twenties or early thirties. He was massive, with light brown hair and broad features. His oversized ears stuck out a bit from his head, and his smile was a little crooked.

He's fucking gorgeous. The random thought made Noah's cheeks heat.

The man spoke, but Noah was too out of it to focus on his lips. The warm weight of the man's hand helped still his trembling, but he couldn't make his dad's text go away.

Noah shook his head. "Can't hear. Sorry." Noah's eyes fell on the phone again, and he shuddered. "He's supposed to be in prison."

The man breathed out, then tried speaking again. He spoke slower this time, but Noah still couldn't concentrate. He had to be paying close attention to speechread, and his mind just couldn't take it right then.

The man pulled a phone from his pocket and typed something, then held it up. *My name is Zed. What can I do to help?*

Noah flushed. "Justin and Griff's brother."

Zed nodded and sat beside him, then wrapped an

arm around Noah's shoulders. He typed on the phone. *You're Noah, right?*

"Yeah." Noah tried to even his breathing and pull himself together. "My dad is supposed to be in prison."

Zed picked up Noah's phone and read the text, anger filling his eyes. His lips moved fast, but Noah thought he was cursing. He typed in his own phone again. *Justin told me some of what they did to your brother and you.*

"The whole town knows," Noah said, sighing. "My parents locked me up in a mental hospital. They wanted my VA benefits." He laughed, the vibration rough in his throat. "Like there was really that much."

I see your dad texted you. I thought you had a restraining order.

Noah looked up from Zed's phone, swallowing hard. "I thought I did too."

We can call my BIL, Tanner. He'll know what to do.

Tanner was a sheriff's deputy and *would* know what to do, but Noah was reluctant to drag the police into this. It was a family thing.

His knee bumped against Zed's as he shifted. It was odd, having a stranger close enough to feel his body heat. It was a little electrifying too. Zed was an attractive man. He was big enough to make Noah feel damn near delicate.

Noah felt his face heat again. "I just need to talk to Caden. He's my lawyer." He took a breath. "I can do this."

Zed smiled his crooked smile, and Noah's heart beat

faster. "Yes, you can." He started to hold his phone up, but Noah stilled him.

"I can speechread pretty well when I'm not out of it. I'm sorry to be such a pain in the ass. Hold on." Noah grabbed his phone and texted Caden. "There. He'll let me know what's going on with them."

Zed gave him an intense look. "You're not a pain in the ass," he said slowly.

Noah made a face. "If you say so. You don't have to speak extra slow or anything. Just make sure you're facing me when you speak. Now, you're here for the sandwich club, aren't you?"

Zed's shoulders shook when he laughed. "Yeah. Peanut, Butter, and Jelly. I have to say it in that order too."

Noah shifted from under Zed's arm and stood. He held his hand out and helped the other man stand. "I'm happy to stable them for as long as you need. They're charming little buggers."

Zed shook his head. "I can't believe I adopted three miniature horses."

Noah laughed. "You might want to stay away from Doc Grover. He knows you're a softy now, and he'll saddle you with all kinds of pets."

Zed scowled. "He played me."

"Yep." Noah opened Peanut's stall, and Zed slipped in to pet the pintaloosa. The other alpha looked up from hugging the miniature. He said something, but Noah didn't catch it.

Zed pointed farther down the row of stalls.

Noah turned around and saw Carrot glaring at him.

"Aww, I'm sorry, buddy. Was I giving these cuties too much attention?"

He went to Carrot's stall and rubbed the pinto's soft nose. He settled his forehead on the horse's neck and breathed in his scent. "Do you forgive me?"

Carrot rubbed his big head against Noah's chest, making him laugh.

A tug on the bottom of his flannel shirt drew his attention. Butter stood behind him, watching them with big, sad eyes.

Carrot nuzzled the top of the miniature's head, making Butter's hat tilt down over his eyes.

Zed jogged over, wincing. "Sorry. I didn't close his gate." He straightened Butter's hat before patting Carrot's neck. "Who's this guy?"

Noah rubbed Carrot's ears. "This is Carrot. He's one of the rescues."

Zed eyes went soft. "He's more than that."

Noah made a face. "Okay, so I love him." He straightened. "That doesn't mean I don't love all my horses. I do, I swear."

"I understand. I'm that way with my plants." Zed spoke clearly, but Noah didn't catch everything he said next. "She's my favorite even if I have a lot of other ferns."

Noah smiled and nodded. *No sense making him explain things over and over again. Don't want to annoy the gorgeous alpha.*

Zed gave him a look. "You didn't understand that one, did you?"

Noah deflated. "No, I'm sorry."

"Don't be. I was confusing." Zed took his phone out. "I named my favorite fern." He held his phone up. *Eugenia.*

Noah laughed, understanding Zed's earlier point. "Eugenia. That's a good fern name. She's special and your favorite even if you love all your plants."

Zed smiled proudly. "Yes. I have pictures."

He showed Noah a few pictures of a bushy fern.

"She's lovely," Noah said politely, trying not to laugh again.

"Janelle gave me an ivy today." Zed held up his phone again. *Maude.*

Noah nodded, face grave. "Now Eugenia has a sister."

Zed grinned. "I know you're joking, but it's true." He patted Butter's neck. "She has two more sisters and a brother too. I just need to build a barn."

"Until then, visit them any time." Noah grabbed a few treats for Carrot. "I live in the house on the creek, so even if we're closed, just come get me, and I'll let you in the barn."

"Thank you," Zed said, smiling softly. "Do you need any help here?"

Noah considered him for a moment. Zed seemed like the kind that liked to stay busy. "Grab the broom over there and start sweeping if you don't mind. I'll get these fellas fed."

Zed gave him a grateful look and moved for the broom.

Noah patted Carrot one more time, then led Butter back to his stall. He quickly fed the horses and refreshed their hay while Zed thoroughly swept the hallway and tack room. It only took a half hour or so, but it was nice having the man around, even if they weren't talking. Maybe *because* they weren't talking.

His phone vibrated, and he took a deep breath before reading the text.

Caden: The restraining orders expired a month ago. I called Nevada, and they've been out of jail for a year and a half now. They both got out for good behavior. First Rachael, then Steven. I'll talk with Sherriff McKenzie and figure out how to renew the restraining order. Keep all of his texts and update me if he contacts you again. Don't engage and DON'T send that fucker a thing.

Noah squeezed his eyes shut. He just wanted them to stay away from him and Elijah.

He jumped when he felt a hand on his arm, then settled down and went easily as Zed pulled him into a hug. The other alpha's scent was soothing and was fast becoming addictive. He hated looking weak in front of the man. He didn't want Zed's pity. *I want him to see me.*

He took a breath and pushed back. "I'm alright. Thank you."

Zed kept ahold of Noah's arms. "It's okay to be upset." The rest of his words were too fast for Noah to read.

Noah sighed, suddenly exhausted. Even with every person around him trying to make communication easier for him, talking was still patchwork at best. "I'm sorry, can you repeat that last part again?"

Zed smiled softly, hands gently running up and

down Noah's arms. "Parents have a way of fucking with our heads."

Noah's laugh felt rough. "That's the truth. I guess I should tell you that I know about your dad too. Justin is basically a Wilson, even if he won't admit it."

Zed snorted. "I'm definitely telling him that." He looked sad for a moment. "My dad was a bigamist and a liar that abandoned his families. Your parents are manipulating narcissists. We make a good pair."

Noah licked his lips. He liked the heat of Zed's hands on his arms. "Yeah. We do."

CHAPTER 4

Zed checked Eugenia's soil. "Looking good, Eugenia. How do you like Maude?"

The English Ivy hung next to Eugenia in the big kitchen window. They looked a little unbalanced, and Zed swore Eugenia pouted at having to share her space.

"Siblings aren't too horrible, sweetheart." He winced. "Well, considering I'm going on a damn date tonight, maybe siblings are horrible."

He looked over his other plants. He had several pots of ivy, succulents, and herbs around the kitchen. *I wonder if Noah needs an aloe plant for his kitchen.*

Over the past few days, he had found himself thinking about the younger alpha often. He stopped by and visited his miniatures every day and ended up helping Noah finish out his evening chores while he was there. Then they jogged a few miles together before Zed forced himself to go home.

Zed enjoyed it a lot more than he should. There was

something about the other man that drew Zed in. He had even started trying to learn ASL from a few sites online. It was going to be hard as hell, but Zed knew it would be worth it. For the first time since moving to Hobson Hills, he wished they were in a larger city so he could take classes instead.

He wanted no barriers between Noah and himself, and while the other alpha was very good at speechreading, Zed didn't want to leave all the work of communicating to him.

Zed washed his hands and grabbed his keys. "I'll see you girls later. Don't worry. I won't be home late. Sam's nice and all, but this is just dinner."

His truck came to a stop at the end of his long driveway, and he thought for a moment. *It won't hurt to stop by Noah's first. He might need someone to walk Carrot.* He turned right instead of left and headed farther away from Hobson Hills.

He pulled into Noah's driveway and drove past the watermill house. Zed loved the place. He'd been inside once now and thought it might be the most peaceful place he'd ever been. The sound of the creek and water wheel lulled him in, and Noah's calm presence made him want to stay.

It could use some more plants, he thought with a smile. He really didn't recall seeing any aloe in the kitchen.

Zed parked next to Noah's truck and jumped out. He knew Noah saved the smaller barn for last, so he slipped inside.

Noah and Dean were tending to the horses near the tack room. Noah's back was to him, and Zed took a moment to admire Noah's wide shoulders and slim hips. The man's curly black hair looked styled. *Hmm, Noah isn't wearing a hat like normal.*

Zed noticed Butter was wearing another cowboy hat and smiled. *There it is.*

He started toward them, grinning at Dean's laughter. The omega was a really nice guy.

"My love for you is like diarrhea. I just can't hold it in," Noah said, hands pressed to his heart. "Will that one win my date over, Dean?"

Dean leaned against Carrot's stall, laughing hard enough that Zed thought the man might wet himself. "Please, use that line. I really want to know how he reacts."

Zed's smile faded, and his eyes narrowed. The idea of Noah going on a date didn't sit well with him. He wasn't sure what the heavy emotion in his chest was, but it wasn't good.

He tapped Noah's arm to get his attention.

Noah's eyes brightened when he saw him. "Zed, I thought you weren't coming by tonight."

Zed shrugged. "I had a little time."

"You look nice," Dean said, brows raised. He looked between Zed and Noah. "You both actually look really nice."

Zed noticed Noah's clean jeans and boots and nice dark green button-down shirt. The color went well with Noah's light brown skin and hazel eyes. The freckles across his nose begged for a kiss, but Zed thought it might be a little *too* weird if he leaned over and kissed Noah's nose. Maybe.

"Do you have plans tonight?" Zed asked, voice rough even to his own ears.

Noah made a face. "I have a date at the Irish Rose tonight."

Zed's eyes widened. "Me too. We should ride together."

Dean blinked. "Ride together to your separate dates?"

"Sure." Zed shrugged. "What time do you have to be there?"

Noah frowned in concentration.

Zed didn't wait for him to ask him to repeat himself. "What time do you have to be there?"

Noah smiled. "Six."

"Perfect. Me too." Zed grabbed a treat from the bin hanging on the wall and fed it to Carrot. "If we finish early enough, we can come back and brush Carrot and the sandwich club."

Noah ran his hands through his black hair. "I'd like that."

Dean shook his head. "You two sound so eager for your dates."

Zed shrugged. "My brothers set me up."

Noah groaned. "Elijah set me up too. Brothers are so annoying."

"Yes, they are." Zed guided Noah toward the barn door. "See you later, Dean."

Dean watched them leave with a strange smirk on his face. "Have fun."

Zed held Noah's door open for him as he climbed

into Zed's truck. He ignored the confused look Noah gave him and shut the door.

The drive to town was quiet, but Zed didn't mind. He hadn't really been around Noah away from the stable, and it felt really nice. The other alpha had a way of looking around him as if he was trying to take everything in all the time.

Zed pulled into the parking lot of the Irish Rose. Noah was out of the truck as soon as Zed put it in park. He had Zed's door open a few seconds later.

Zed laughed as he got out. "Thanks."

The pub was busy, but it was early evening on a Friday, so that was to be expected. North and Wiley were tending the bar, and Laura and a few other servers were darting back and forth from the kitchen to the tables.

Zed waved at Sam when he saw him. The omega had a table by the window.

"You're on a date with Sam?" Noah asked, voice a little louder than he likely intended it to be.

Zed nodded. "Yeah. Want to come sit with us?"

Noah bit his lip. "I don't see my date here yet. Elijah said his name was Joey. He's blond with blue eyes and should be wearing a blue and grey sweater. I have his picture on my phone."

Zed pulled Noah with him. He made sure he faced him when he spoke. "We'll watch for him from the table."

Sam jumped up and hugged Noah. "It's good to see you again, Noah." He signed something, making Noah laugh.

Zed scowled and sat across from Sam. It was stupid to feel jealous that Sam could sign while he couldn't.

"I'm sorry, Sam." Noah smiled shyly. "Zed invited me to wait for my date here. Do you mind?"

"Not at all."

Noah sat beside Zed. "I'm sure I'll be gone soon, and you two can have your date."

Sam gave Zed a playful look. "I think Zed and I both know this isn't going anywhere."

Zed smiled apologetically. "I'm sorry my brothers roped you into this."

"Why wouldn't you want to date Zed?" Noah sounded a little angry. "He's a great guy, and he's hot. Look at his ears." Noah poked Zed's ear. "They're adorable."

Zed felt his face heat up. *Noah thinks I'm hot?*

Sam rubbed his chin, dark eyes full of mischief. "Now that you mention it, Zed is really hot. Maybe I'm not thinking this through."

Noah scowled and crossed his arms. "He's not *that* good-looking. You're better off without him."

Zed leaned back and studied Noah's face. He knew Sam didn't have any interest in him. The two had gotten to know each other the last couple of weeks. He was just doing this as a favor to Justin. Noah, however, didn't know that.

"Are you jealous?" Zed asked Noah. "Do you like Sam?"

Sam snorted and coke dripped from his nose. "Damn it." He grabbed a tissue.

Noah looked confused. "Sam is a wonderful guy, but we're just friends."

Sam looked between them and grinned around the tissue pressed to his nose. "Why don't we order some appetizers. I'm hungry."

Noah looked puzzled, so Zed repeated Sam's words since the omega's hands were busy. Noah gave him a grateful look.

They spent the next hour eating and talking. Noah watched the door, but with each minute that passed, he seemed to get sadder.

Sam patted Noah's hand. "Did you really want to date the man?"

Noah made a face. "No, but it sucks that he didn't show up. I need a drink."

Zed wanted to hug the other alpha but knew it wouldn't be appreciated at the moment. "I'm glad he didn't come. I'm having fun."

Sam chuckled. "Me too. I don't want to date either of you, but it's nice to hang out."

"You should come visit the sandwich club." Zed took a bite of his Reuben sandwich. Albie was the evening cook, and while he wasn't Reuben, he still made a good sandwich.

Sam tilted his head, eyeing him with curiosity. "Huh?"

Noah's wide smile showed off the little gap between his front teeth, and Zed's breath caught, making him choke.

Noah patted his back, then turned to Sam. "Zed

here adopted three miniature horses named Peanut, Butter, and Jelly."

Sam looked surprised. "Really? Wait. I really shouldn't be surprised at the names. Justin's rabbit is named Butter Bunny. I think the Ames family likes butter."

Zed watched Noah as the younger man told Sam all about Zed's minis. Noah loved horses. He'd seen it over the past few days, but the man fucking lit up when he talked about them. Zed thought it was possibly the hottest thing he'd ever seen.

What the hell is wrong with me? Zed wasn't the type to wax poetic over anyone. His exes had often complained he was too blunt and pragmatic for romance.

Zed sipped his ice water. He might be romantically challenged, but he wasn't stupid. He hadn't wanted someone this much in a long time, if ever. Now, all he had to do was convince Noah to be his.

Noah was a little tipsy when they left the Irish Rose. The date he hadn't really wanted had ghosted him. What was worse was that Zed knew it.

Noah wasn't that worried about what Sam thought, but he did care what Zed thought about him. *Now he probably thinks I'm a sad loser.*

He stumbled and Zed wrapped an arm around his waist. Noah couldn't resist leaning into him and sniffing the man's neck. He smelled so damn good. He always did.

He felt Zed's laughter shaking his body.

Zed helped him into the truck and buckled his seatbelt for him. *He definitely thinks I'm a loser,* Noah thought.

Zed patted his knee, then shut Noah's door.

Noah curled into the seat and closed his eyes. Alcohol always made him sleepy. He had learned to avoid drinking at poker night with his buddies. "If I drink too much, Niccolo gets all my money. He's a sneaky little bastard."

Zed patted his arm and pulled out of the parking lot.

Noah opened his eyes and watched the evening shadows dance across Zed's face. "I wish I could flirt. Even before losing my hearing, I was shitty at dating. Of course, Mom and Dad only let me date girls in high school, so that was a problem. They thought omegas were wastes of space, and there was no way they'd accept me being gay anyway."

Zed frowned and said something, but it was too dark for Noah to read his lips.

"I like your lips." Noah pursed his own. "They look so soft, and when you smile your crooked smile, I lose my train of thought."

Zed smiled.

"Just like that." Noah rubbed his face against the leather seat. "Mind blown."

Noah was almost asleep by the time they pulled into his driveway. Zed helped him out of the truck and walked him to the house.

Noah leaned into him and sniffed his neck again. "Why do you always smell so good? Do you roll in peppermint and lemon?"

Zed's body shook with laughter again. Noah liked it when the other alpha laughed. He got the impression Zed didn't laugh enough.

Noah unlocked his door, and Zed helped him inside. He fell down on the couch and pulled Zed with him.

Noah leaned back against the arm and watched Zed for a minute. "I'm not a loser."

Zed frowned. "I know."

"I'm a little messed up, but Diane helped me work through a lot when I moved to Hobson Hills."

"I like Diane." Zed smiled.

"Yeah, she's great." Noah rested his head on the back of the couch. "She says I worry about having my control taken away again. Sometimes I dream about being tied down and drugged again, and I wake up screaming. That's only sometimes though."

Zed moved closer on the couch until his knees bumped Noah's. He eyes flashed with anger when he spoke. "Your parents will never take you away again. You have people to protect you now." He made the sign for *protect*. "You're not alone."

Noah smiled softly. "You signed."

Zed's cheeks pinkened. "I'm learning ASL from an online teacher Diane suggested. It's hard. It's a whole new language, and I didn't realize facial expressions could be so important."

Noah snorted. "I know, right? I think the only reason I learned as fast as I did is because of Olive. She made friends online in the Deaf community and really pushed me to learn ASL instead of just Signed English. She said it wasn't enough to just get by. I needed to flourish. Now she's teaching the twins ASL too."

Noah smiled softly. He used his voice to express himself, but communication was a two-way street, and he enjoyed being able to have full, deep conversations with his family and friends. Olive and Elijah had also been the ones to introduce him to Diane. *I owe them so much.*

"You love Olive and the twins." Zed gave him an understanding look. "I love my nieces too."

"They're special." Noah breathed out slowly, eyes feeling heavy. "You're special too, Zed. I don't want you to think I'm a loser."

Zed shook his head, and his hands made the sign for *brave.*

Noah smiled happily and fell asleep.

A FEW DAYS LATER, ZED SEALED THE FERMENTER ON THE newest batch of A&J's Pale Ale. It had been a long day, but Abel had wanted to get a little ahead since he would be going on paternity leave soon. This week was going to be a lot of work, but Zed found he didn't mind too much.

Abel watched him from his office doorway. "You've been quiet this week. Well, quieter than usual."

Zed gave him a considering look. "Noah."

Abel nodded, face confused. "He's my cousin."

Zed grabbed the broom from the corner and started sweeping. He had swept after lunch, but it wouldn't hurt to do it again. "I like him."

"He's a good guy." Abel yawned and stretched his arms over his head. "Noah had it rough with his shitty parents, but we've taken care of him since he's moved here. I just made a date for him for next Saturday. My friend Mason has had the hots for him forever."

The broom handle made an odd crunching noise when Zed squeezed it a little too hard. Abel and he both stared at the broken handle in surprise. The silence between them stretched toward awkwardness, and Zed shuffled his feet, face heating with embarrassment.

Abel pressed his hands to his cheeks, eyes widening in excitement. "Did my pragmatic and stoic right-hand man just throw a jealous fit? When you say you *like* Noah, do mean you want to slob his knob?"

Zed shuddered. "What the hell is wrong with you? Slob his knob?"

Abel winced. "I may have been looking words up on urban dictionary. Valentina will be dating before we know it, and I want to be prepared."

"Would she even call a blowjob that?"

"I don't know." Abel rolled his eyes. "That's why I'm looking things up. Now answer the question."

Zed rubbed his face. "What was the question again?"

Abel giggled. "Do you want to do the nasty with my cousin?"

For some reason, Abel's urban dictionary slang reminded Zed of Noah's corny pickup lines and made him smile. "I want to date him."

Abel gave him a considering look. "I always pictured Noah with a sweet omega that he could take care of. Instead, *you* want to take care of *him*."

Zed frowned, shaking his head. "No, I don't. Noah doesn't need anyone to take care of him. He's one of the most capable people I know."

Abel gave him a smug look. "Good answer. It's too late to cancel the date with Mason, so I'll call in a favor from Sam, and you all can make it a double date so you can keep an eye on them. You had better work fast. Grammy and Aunt Anna are making a list of omegas. I'll try to stall them."

"Thanks," Zed said, smiling. "Now, maybe you should get out of here before Mateo comes and drags you home." The two had gotten married over the weekend, but were waiting until after their baby was born to go on the honeymoon. Mateo was a bit overprotective at the moment.

Abel grinned. "I kinda like it when he gets all caveman and parks the beef bus."

Zed made a face and threw his hands up. "I'm out of here. I'm meeting Griff for dinner. Do Valentina a favor and stop expanding your slang."

Thirty minutes later, he parked outside the Kozy Kitchen. It felt strange not to eat at the Irish Rose, but Griff had said he was craving gravy and biscuits.

Zed ran through the rain and ducked into the diner. Griff gave him a pitiful wave from the back booth, making Zed pause a moment.

He studied his little brother carefully. Griff was paler than usual and looked worn out. Bea wasn't there either. That meant she was either with Justin or her babysitter, Ines.

"Have you been working too much again?" he asked, sliding into the booth.

Griff shrugged, not bothering to argue. "I need to work while I can."

Zed's eyes narrowed. "What the hell does that mean? Are they laying you off or something?"

Griff climbed out of his booth and slid in beside Zed. "Hug me."

He didn't hesitate to pull his brother into a tight hug. "What's wrong?"

"First, I need you to promise not to tell anyone, not even Justin. Everyone will know soon enough, but we want to keep it to ourselves for as long as possible."

Zed's fists clenched in the back of Griff's sweater. "Griff, what the hell is wrong?"

"You know Luke, right?"

Zed rolled his eyes. "Yes, I recall your best friend. Explain the problem, Griff. I'll fix it."

Griff leaned back, smiling softly. "You like to take care of everyone. Okay, so Luke and I fooled around a little."

Zed growled, eyes narrowing. "I'll kill him."

Griff punched his arm. "For what? We were both lonely and blew off some steam. It was no big deal."

"Clearly it's a big deal." Zed tried to unclench his jaw. "What did he do?"

"*We* got pregnant," Griff said, voice tired. "One night a couple of months ago, Marie called and told me Bill and his new omega just had a huge baby shower. She said he was all excited about the baby and making this big deal out of it."

Zed cursed. Griff's ex hadn't wanted kids. When Griff had gotten pregnant with Bea, Bill had made it clear they were over.

"I was depressed and lonely. Luke was pining after

Brittney. She was dating Tommy at the time, so he thought he didn't stand a chance with her. We comforted one another."

"He's dating Brittney now," Zed said, voice hard. "I'll have a talk with him."

"No." Griff flicked his ear. "No talks needed. Luke and I have already talked. We're going to raise this baby together, but *not* as a couple. We don't feel that way about one another, and it would ruin our friendship, which would do a lot more harm than good."

"Bullshit," Zed said, scowling.

"Is it?" Griff arched a brow. "Would it be better to force ourselves into a relationship we don't want for the sake of the baby?"

Zed deflated. "No, damn it. I have some money saved and you have insurance. We can do this."

"Yes, *we* can," Griff said, hugging him. "I never doubted for one moment that you'd help me. I really hoped you wouldn't kill Luke, but I knew you'd offer to take care of everything." He leaned back. "Here's the thing. I don't want your savings account, Zed. I just want you to be there for me."

Zed squeezed him tight, pressing his face against Griff's hair. "I'll always be here for you and Bea. The new baby too. Hell, even fucking Luke, but only after I kick his ass a couple of times."

"Zed." Griff chuckled. "No hurting Luke."

Zed sniffed. "Just a little ass kicking. Nothing too permanent. I'll get Noah to go with me. He has a way of keeping me sensible."

Griff gave him a knowing look. "You talk a lot about Noah. How are the ASL classes going?"

Zed scowled again. "Don't change the subject. When are you telling Justin?"

"Give me a couple of weeks." Griff made a face. "Luke has to tell his parents too. The whole town will know then."

"Small towns." Zed leaned back, wrapping an arm around Griff. "Let's get you some biscuits and gravy and start planning. I missed Bea's birth, but I'm not going to miss this one."

Griff sighed and leaned his head on Zed's shoulder. "I love you."

"Love you too."

He shot Zed a mischievous look. "I'm going to have to learn sign language, aren't I?"

"Make it ASL," Zed said, frowning at the menu. "Noah prefers it."

CHAPTER 6

"I can't believe Elijah and Abel wouldn't let me out of this." Noah scowled as he watched Zed do another few reps of squat thrusts. His friend couldn't stand being still for long, and they'd been waiting on their *dates* for fifteen minutes.

Zed did one more rep and hopped up. "It's just one date, and Sam and I will be here too."

Zed's three miniatures watched him curiously, eyes and heads following their person's movements. Butter wore a navy blue, knitted toboggan, and Peanut and Jelly both had their own knit caps and colorful barrettes.

Carrot settled his head over Noah's shoulder, so he leaned against his horse and scratched his nose. "I've known Mason for a year. It's not happening."

Zed was the one scowling this time. "Damn right, it isn't."

Noah frowned, certain he misunderstood. "Can you repeat that?"

Zed gave him an innocent look and batted his eyes. "I can't remember what I said."

"From two seconds ago?" Noah arched a brow.

Zed shrugged and checked the gas gauge on the two ATVs.

"I think I'll text Justin and tell him you really want a cat." Noah slowly pulled his phone from his back pocket and laughed at Zed's panicked expression.

"Why would you do that to me?" Zed's bottom lip trembled, and Noah shoved him before putting his phone away.

Zed's head turned toward the road, and Noah followed his gaze. A small, lime green car pulled in and parked next to Zed's truck. Zed moved to stand next to Noah, arms crossed and a distinctly grumpy expression on his broad face.

Sam and Mason got out, both bundled up in warm clothes. The late October air was a bit cold, but it was a rare beautiful, clear day.

Mason waved and gave him a wide smile.

Okay? Noah smiled back hesitantly. Normally, Mason was really shy around Noah, but at that moment, the omega looked on the verge of laughter as he looked between Noah and Zed.

Sam gave Mason a knowing look. "See? I told you."

"I hate that I'm too late," Mason said, pouting.

"You all aren't too late," Noah said, trying to smooth things over. "We have plenty of sunshine left in the day. Let me put the horses up, and we'll get on the trail."

Mason giggled, and Sam rolled his eyes, while Zed just flushed and looked up at the blue sky.

Noah patted Zed's arm. "Z made lunch. He's a really good cook and made ham and potato soup. We also packed some warm blankets. Prepare to be wowed by the natural beauty around us." He shot finger guns toward Zed. "Just be warned, if Zed was a transformer, he'd be Optimus Fine. Try not to fall in love while I'm gone."

Zed's crooked grin was worth Noah's heated cheeks as Mason and Sam leaned into one another and laughed.

Noah pulled Carrot's lead and whistled. "Come on Peanut, Butter, and Jelly. Back to the barn."

The three miniatures trotted behind him, and he risked a glance back at Zed. The alpha watched him with soft eyes.

Noah leaned into Carrot when they entered the barn. "I can't believe I said that. Zed just looked so uncomfortable, and I didn't want him to feel awkward. He probably thinks I'm an idiot now. *I* think I'm an idiot."

Carrot butted his head against Noah's shoulder.

"You're right. It's not like I stand a chance with him anyway. Mason is nice, I guess." Noah sighed and put Carrot and the miniatures in their stalls.

Butter watched him with longing.

"I'm sorry, big guy. You can't keep up with the ATVs." Noah patted his head and snuck him a treat.

By the time he shut the barn door behind him, the other three were ready to go. Noah blinked uncertainly at Mason and Sam. The sat together on one of the ATVs, while Zed took the other. *That's not how it's supposed to go. Zed and Sam ride one, and Mason and I ride the other.*

Zed patted the seat behind him and grinned. "We're ready."

Noah shrugged and climbed behind Zed. *I'd rather cuddle with Zed anyway.* He tugged Zed's cap down around his ears, then did the same with his own. Then he wrapped his arms around Zed's waist and didn't even try to keep distance between them. He hugged Zed and settled his chin on the other alpha's shoulder.

Noah enjoyed the vibrations of the ATV thrumming beneath him and the crisp fall air as they drove through the woods. *This is the perfect date. No talking, no crowds. Just a nice day with Zed.* He breathed deeply, enjoying the appealing scent of the alpha in front of him. *Perfect.*

A few hours later, they came to a stop at a clearing near Marco and Bennett's house. Noah reluctantly untangled himself from around Zed and slid off the ATV. His legs wobbled a bit, so he took a minute to stretch.

Mason did his own stretching and smiled at him. "This is so much fun. Thank you for inviting me out, Noah. I hope we can be friends, and do this more often."

And I'm friend zoned, Noah thought, strangely happy about it. "That would be great."

Sam and Zed spread a couple of the blankets on the ground, and they settled in a circle. Noah passed everyone cups, and Zed poured soup into them from the thermos they had brought.

"Okay," Sam said. "Let me tell you all what North told Griff yesterday when he came into the pub for lunch."

"Oh, no." Zed snorted a laugh. "Why does his foot get stuck in his mouth every time Griff comes around?"

Noah settled onto his side and let himself enjoy the day.

A COUPLE OF DAYS LATER, ZED PACED THE FLOOR IN THE waiting room of the regional hospital. Justin had been in labor for six hours. "Do you think everything is alright?"

"Sometimes babies take time." Griff sat with Bea and watched as she colored in one of her many coloring books. "First babies especially."

Zed tugged at the collar of his shirt, unsure exactly why he was nervous. He really wished Noah was there.

Abel and Justin's two other best friends, Caden and Grey, waited with them.

Grey gave Zed an exasperated look. "You need to calm down before you make yourself sick."

"Seriously, Zed," Abel said, hands propped on his pregnant belly. "You're going to pass out."

"Justin's in good hands. It'll be alright," Caden said gravely.

"I'm okay. I'm just a little on edge. No problem. There's absolutely no problem here." He ran his hands through his hair. "Justin is good. It's just a baby."

The elevator dinged, then opened, and Noah stepped out and looked around until he saw him.

Zed stopped pacing and released a pent-up breath. "Noah."

Noah smiled wide and held up the oversized stuffed bear he carried. "Where's the baby?"

Zed scowled. "She's not here yet. It shouldn't take this long, right?"

"For fuck's sake," Abel muttered and rolled his eyes.

Noah shrugged. "Elijah took almost twenty-four hours to deliver the twins. Grammy says sometimes babies take a while."

Zed smiled, relieved. "That's good to know."

Griff snorted and handed Bea another crayon.

Noah patted Zed's back and handed him the bear. "Have a seat, Uncle Z. I'll go get you a bottle of water."

Zed sat down with the bear in his lap and watched Noah walk toward the vending machines.

The four men in the room gave him the same pointed look.

"What?" he asked, jumping back up and doing a couple reps of burpees.

Noah came back and handed Zed the water and waited for him to take a drink. "Okay, let's see how long it takes you to do twenty reps."

The next hour passed quickly with Noah there. By the time Tanner came to the waiting room, Zed was worn out, but calm.

Tanner grinned, eyes wet with tears. "Justin and baby Rhonda are doing well. They cleaned her up and have her fed. Justin wants to see you guys before he falls asleep. Griff, Bea, and Zed first."

Noah grabbed Zed's shoulders and shook him from his daze. "Go meet your new niece."

Zed shared a grin with his friend and grabbed the bear. "I'm telling Justin I brought this."

Noah shook his head, eyes soft. "Get moving."

Zed gave him one last look and followed Tanner, Griff, and Bea down the hallway. Bea grinned at him over Griff's shoulder, and Zed blew her a kiss. *I wish I had been here for Bea's birth.*

Justin sat up in bed with a little yellow bundle in his arms. He laughed when he saw the bear. "I can't believe you all waited for so long."

Zed set the bear in one of the chairs. "We're your family. We wanted to be here for you and meet Ronnie."

Justin's face screwed up, and he started to sob.

Tanner gave them a panicked look and sat on the bed to hug Justin. "Hey now, why the tears, love?"

"I have brothers," Justin managed to say through his tears. "I have a family."

Griff wiped his own eyes and hugged Justin from his other side. "We love you, Justin. Zed and I are so happy you let us be part of your life."

Zed sat at the end of the bed and patted Justin's foot. He couldn't speak easily past the lump in his throat. It had always been him and Griff against the world. He couldn't imagine trying to go it alone as a kid. "We're here, Justin."

After a little while, Justin's tears slowed, and he gave them an embarrassed look. "I'm sorry, guys."

"Never apologize for feeling," Zed said softly. He may have only met Justin a few months ago, but he loved the other man as much as he did Griff. "Family comforts."

Bea patted Justin's cheek. "Kiss the baby?"

Justin chuckled. "Oh, honey bee. Come meet your cousin."

Zed turned around to share a smile with Noah, then remembered he wasn't there. *Damn it, I want my alpha.* Some moments were meant to be shared, and Noah was quickly becoming one of the most important people in Zed's life.

CHAPTER 7

DECEMBER

*N*oah rubbed his eyes as he opened his door to find Elijah and the kids on his front porch. "Why are you all here so early?"

Snow poured outside, and Noah was happy to be in the warm house. It was the first snowstorm of the season, and he was a little worried about Jake making it to work that morning. It was Saturday, so usually Jake and he were the only ones taking care of the horses.

I'm not worried that Zed won't come by today. Not. At. All.

It had been over a month since his date with Mason, and while he'd enjoyed it, he was quite happy that everyone had stopped trying to set him up with random omegas. He suspected they thought he was sad about Joey ghosting him and Mason friend zoning him.

Noah felt only slightly guilty that he hadn't corrected anyone. Despite what he had told everyone, he suddenly had very little interest in dating an omega. He had a slight obsession with a big-eared alpha.

Zed came to visit his horses every day, then spent the evening hanging out with Noah before heading home for the night. Noah fucking loved it. Every second he spent with the man was a complete joy.

Elijah gave him a curious look and tapped his arm to get his attention. "Where did your mind go?"

Noah scowled at his brother but couldn't keep it up when Connor and Cooper each hugged one of his legs. His nephews were too stinking cute for their own good. They smiled their gap-toothed smiles, and Noah knew he'd let them all inside. He mentally rolled his eyes at himself. *Like you wouldn't have anyway.*

Olive bounced in place, a wide smile covering her face as she signed. "Daddy has a surprise, Uncle Noah."

"Are you making me pancakes?" Noah asked hopefully.

Elijah held up the brown bag in his arm. "Fresh apple pancakes with maple syrup."

"Please, come in." Noah opened the door wide and the four pushed inside. Make that five. Hotdog was with them.

Carter's hairy Old English Sheep dog licked his hand as he passed.

"Are we still on for our sleepover Wednesday, Olive?" Noah asked.

His niece only had a few days left in school before the winter break, and she had already told him they were celebrating with a Harry Potter movie marathon. Fortunately, she didn't mind watching the movies with the subtitles on, and he'd gotten used to his new normal.

"Yes!" She fist bumped him on her way to the living room with the twins.

Elijah wiggled in place before setting the bag down and pulling out his ingredients. "I have some important news."

Noah sat at one of the stools lining the counter. "You're pregnant."

Elijah stopped dancing and pouted. "It was supposed to be a surprise."

"Then you shouldn't glow so much when you're pregnant." Noah shrugged. "I noticed a couple of weeks ago. Then, a few days ago, when Carter was all protective alpha at Rue's birthday party, I knew for sure."

Elijah sulked and washed some apples, then grabbed a knife. "You could have at least acted surprised. Carter's telling his parents and brothers now."

Noah's mouth made an O and he slapped his cheeks. "Oh my god, Elijah! You're pregnant?"

Elijah stopped slicing apples to point his sharp knife at Noah. "Watch your tone, little brother."

Noah laughed and stole an apple slice. "Sorry. I really am happy for you two. You guys are the best parents."

"You're the best uncle." Elijah's smile faded. "No more messages from Steven or Rachael?"

"No." Noah made a face. "Hopefully they stay gone. There's not a lot we can do unless they threaten us."

"I think they'll just move on to some other scheme." Elijah's words came fast, and Noah didn't catch them all, but he caught enough. "There's no welcome for them here, and they know it."

"I hope so." Noah didn't want to talk about their parents. It just made him itchy inside. "I rode Carrot yesterday. He handles well and is really gentle. He'll be a good therapy horse."

Elijah grinned. "You just love him and don't want to adopt him out."

"I'll give him a good home." Noah wrinkled his nose. "Zed said if I tried to sell him, he'd throw me in a horse trough."

"Zed," Elijah said slowly, drawing the name out and signing the letters to add emphasis. He resumed cutting his apples. "All I hear from you anymore is 'Zed said this' or 'Zed did that.' I think someone has a crush on a brown-eyed alpha."

Noah looked around. "Did we somehow transport back to high school. Please tell me it isn't so."

Elijah pointed his knife again. "You should ask Zed out. I still haven't met the man, but the way you talk about him is enough to know you have it bad."

Noah gave him a suspicious look. "Is that why you're not pushing me to date again?"

Elijah shrugged. "Maybe."

"It doesn't matter. I've decided I'm not dating anymore." Noah shrugged. "I'm too much work."

"I hate that you think that. Joey better watch his back." Elijah put his apples in a pan on the stove and added his spices. He turned around, making sure to face Noah. "I gave him the chance to date the most amazing alpha in the world, and he didn't show up. Fuck him."

Noah chuckled. "Love you too. You know I'm right though. Zed can have any person he wants. There's no way he'll want me. We're friends, but that's all we'll ever be."

And honestly, if Noah couldn't have Zed, then he didn't want anyone. He knew the right person would fit into his life just fine. He just desperately wanted that person to be Zed.

"What you're saying is that I can start arranging dates for you again," Elijah said. "I'll let Zoe, Grammy, and Aunt Anna know."

Noah glared at him. "I'm going to watch cartoons with Hotdog and the kids."

LATER THAT DAY, NOAH FINISHED LAYING DOWN FRESH bedding in Carrot's stall, the smell of straw and shavings filling the air. His horse's new stall was right next to Jelly's, and he was now officially part of the sandwich club.

The three miniatures had gotten new stalls too. Zed wasn't in any hurry to build his barn, so Noah and Carter modified a few of the stalls to make the gates shorter. Now, the three troublemakers could watch over the barn with ease.

He led Carrot back into his new stall and shut the gate. Carrot grabbed his shirt before he could move to the next stall, so Noah took a minute to settle the gelding with gentle pets and a couple of hugs. *Spoiled horse.*

Movement caught his eye, and Noah turned to stare at Jake. The boy rinsed Butter's stallmat while the miniature watched him curiously, which wasn't unusual. What *was* unusual was Jake's behavior. Jake knew Signed English and was very aware that Noah needed to actually see his lips to speechread.

Noah narrowed his eyes in irritation when Jake's mouth moved even though his face was turned toward Butter. The young omega peeked at Noah, then spoke to Butter again.

Noah hid a smile and felt his frustration drain away. Sometimes, Jake had something to say but had trouble saying it. Last time, he had wanted Noah's advice about taking advanced placement classes his freshman year of high school. He had no idea why Jake thought Noah had all the answers, but he wasn't about to turn him away when he needed to talk.

Jake snuck him a look again, and Noah set his pitchfork aside. "Okay, what's going on?"

Apparently, Noah spoke too softly because Jake gave him a confused look. Noah repeated himself, doing his best to adjust his volume. It was always a crapshoot as to whether he'd be successful or not.

Jake's shoulders slumped, and he turned around to face Noah. "Do you think Jared is hot?"

Noah stared at him a moment, sure he'd misunderstood. "Can you repeat that?"

"Jared." Jake signed the rest. "Is he attractive?"

"He's a patient." Noah shrugged. "I can't say I really notice if he's attractive or not. He's just Jared."

Jake hopped up to sit on Carrot's gate, and the horse settled his head over the boy's shoulder. "Jared and I took a picture with Stinkbug last week."

"I remember." Noah smiled. Jared had really come out of his shell since he started working with Stinkbug. He got along well with Jake and the others too. Now, Diane and he came twice a week for their therapy sessions, and Jared came one extra day by himself.

Jake frowned. "I showed my friend Kyle at school, and he went on and on about how hot Jared is."

"Okay?" Noah shrugged. "He thought Jared was hot."

"I don't." Jake gave him a frustrated look. "I don't think anyone is hot. I don't care about… I want to do is hang with my friends. That's it."

It took a minute for Noah to fill in the words he missed since Jake was so shaken.

Noah gave Jake a baffled look. "I don't see what the problem is." Jake's lip trembled, and Noah panicked. "Shit. Okay, whatever it is, we can fix it."

Jake didn't get emotional. Ever. The kid was a steady rock just like his papa.

Jake blinked away tears. "I think I'm broken. I don't want the same stuff all my friends do. I'm not like Jimmy and Jackson either."

Noah had an idea of what he meant. Two of Jake's older brothers were bisexual, while Jake wasn't interested in dating anyone.

Noah gave Jake an awkward hug. "Talk to me. I know you're not broken."

Jake leaned back and gave him a sad look. "I'm not like everyone else. I don't obsess over sex or even want to date anyone. I have zero interest in it all. Zero!" His eyes widened at the last word, and he looked like he was about to pass out.

"Okay." Noah nodded understandingly. "You're definitely not alone in that. There are plenty of people out there who don't care about sex."

Jake looked away. "I don't want to be a freak."

Noah nodded again. *Fuck, I probably look like a bobblehead. Why isn't Ray or Dean here?* "You know my cousin Harper is demisexual. It's a thing. You don't have to be like anyone else. All you have to do is be honest and accept yourself."

"Harper still has Grey." Jake gave him a stubborn look. "He's still married, and he dated before. I don't want that."

Noah sighed. "I just said you don't have to be like anyone else. That includes Harper. If you don't want to date or get married, then don't date or get married. Why are you even thinking about marrying someone?"

When Noah was Jake's age, he'd been doing his best not to think about his romantic future. He had known he was gay, but there was no way his parents would have been okay with it. He hadn't been thinking about marriage and kids or any of that stuff.

"Won't Papa and Dad be mad?" Jake bit his lip. "They told all us kids that all they want is for each of us to be happy and loved."

Noah made a face. "Then what's the problem? You can be happy and loved without sex or a romantic relationship."

"Are you happy without it all?" Jake asked, looking hopeful. "You've seemed happier lately."

Noah winced. "My happiness has nothing to do with yours, Jake." He looked around, then leaned forward. "Besides, I'm happier because of Zed."

Jake blinked for a moment, then grinned. "You like him?"

"Yeah, but don't tell anyone." Noah looked down when Butter tugged on his beltloop. "Silly horse. You need a treat, don't you?"

Jake's grin faded. "Can I be happy without all that stupid romantic stuff?"

Noah rubbed his chin. "I think you can, but one thing I *know* is you won't be happy if you try to be someone you're not."

Jake blew out a breath. "I looked something up online."

Noah had a feeling he knew what was coming. "What did you find?"

"I think I'm asexual and aromantic." Jake swallowed hard and made the sign for *asexual*. "I just said that aloud, didn't I?"

Noah grinned. "Yes, you did. You signed it too. How do you feel about it?"

Jake looked uncertain. "I don't know."

He hugged Jake. "I'm proud of you, kid. You said you looked things up, so you know there are other people out there like you."

"What if I'm wrong?" Jake looked panicked. "What if I'm really something else?"

Noah gasped and hugged Jake tightly. "Maybe you're really a space alien."

Jake pulled away and scowled. "I'm serious."

"Fuck, Jake, if you discover later on that you identify differently, that's okay. Labels really are just labels. They can help you feel like you're not alone, but they're not meant to fence you in. Five years from now, if you discover that you're demi or maybe you're not aromatic, then that's okay. It's okay that you *are* asexual and aromantic too. Your family isn't going to police you about it."

Holy shit, that sounded mature and wise. Noah mentally patted himself on the back.

Jake sighed. "It feels really important."

Noah rubbed his hands over Jake's head, ruffling his hair. "That's because it is. You're figuring out who you are." He turned Jake back to Butter's stall. "I'm telling you right now, you have good dads. They'll understand and support you."

Jake looked over his shoulder, eyes sad. "Your parents didn't support you, did they?"

Noah suddenly felt very tired. "No. They have a shit load of prejudices. They abandoned Elijah when he was born an omega, and they would have done the same to me if I had told them I'm gay, even if I am an alpha."

"Papa and Dad love me." Anger flashed across Jake's face. "Your parents should have loved you too."

"Yeah, they should have." Noah led Peanut from her stall. "Sometimes I wish I would have told them. They would have sent me to Gramps and Grammy, and that would have been better than living with them."

"Marco could have been your dad," Jake said, patting Butter's flanks.

Noah snorted. "He already says he is."

Jake looked to the door, body tensed, then relaxed and waved. "Hey, Zed."

Noah fought the shiver making its way down his back and turned around. Zed leaned against the barn door. The alpha looked delicious in his worn jeans and battered winter coat. His big ears were covered by a thick winter hat.

Zed smiled his sexy, crooked smile. "Jake, your dad's waiting in the Jeep."

Jake pulled his phone out. "Dang it, I didn't realize it had gotten so late. Thanks, Zed." He started for the door, then stopped and turned around. "Thanks, Noah. For everything."

Noah pulled Jake's beanie down around his ears. "No problem, kid. See you tomorrow." Now that the schools were beginning their winter break, Jake would be at Noah's ranch every day.

Jake grinned and ran for the door.

Noah waited until he was gone, then narrowed his eyes on Zed. "You aren't covered in snow. How long were you standing there?"

Zed gave him a soft look and moved closer. "Long enough. You're a good person, Noah. I'm sorry your parents were shit."

Noah shrugged. "Come clean out Peanut's stall while I finish up with Butter's. Jelly is all set to go."

The little black and white miniature shook her head when she heard her name.

"I like the flowers in her hair," Zed said, attempting to sign. He wasn't very good at it yet, but he was learning.

Noah nodded. "It's all part of the Wilson Stables experience."

Zed laughed, and they worked together to finish Noah's chores.

Noah led Butter into his stall, then shut the gate. Butter gave him a disgruntled look and swished his tail before munching his hay.

He watched Zed shovel damp bedding into the wheelbarrow for a moment and mulled on his thoughts. Noah had felt a little off since his visit with Elijah that morning, and he wasn't sure why.

Zed shot him a look over his shoulder, then turned around. "What's going on in that head of yours?"

"Elijah is pregnant," Noah blurted out. "He came by this morning and told me. He's all excited, and Carter and him are happy."

Zed frowned and set his pitchfork down. "Why aren't you happy?"

Noah made a face. "Because I'm an asshole?"

Zed shook his head, eyes narrowed. "What's the real answer?"

"I'm jealous as hell." Noah groaned and leaned against Butter's gate. "Elijah has Carter and three great kids. Now he gets another one while I have nothing." He eyed Zed. "Still think I'm a good person?"

Zed gave him a knowing look. "Yes, I do. There's a

reason Jake talks to you about important things. Plus, I've seen you with Olive. One day, you'll be a great dad. It's okay to be a great uncle until then. Hell, you're still really young, Noah."

Noah shrugged, taking a moment to process Zed's words. "Maybe, but sometimes I want what Elijah and Carter have. Harper was younger than me when Grey had Rue. Hell, I don't even really know if I *do* want kids. I just want a family of my own."

What Noah didn't say was that he had been fine before he met Zed. Now, all he could think about was creating a life with Zed in particular, kids or no kids. They could be a family. *Slow down, Noah,* he reminded himself. *You can't even ask him on a date, but you're planning the wedding.*

Zed leaned forward. "I understand how you feel a little too well. You know Griff's best friend Luke?"

Noah leaned on Peanut's gate and let her slobber all over his hand looking for treats. He nodded. "He's dating some girl named Brittney now, right?"

There had been a lot of talk around town about Griff, Jackson, and Luke. It was a little unusual for an alpha to be besties with two omegas, though people ought to be used to it by now. Noah's friend Caden was best friends with three omegas. Of course, the alpha also carried his pet rabbit strapped to his chest like a baby, so maybe people just thought he was weird.

Worry pulled at the corners of Zed's mouth. "Don't say anything. We haven't even told Justin yet, so I really shouldn't say anything, but it's all I can think of lately."

"Okay." Noah crossed his arms. "I can keep a secret."

"Luke got Griff pregnant," Zed said, scowling. "He fucked him, and now he's dating someone else, and I'm so damn pissed."

Noah scowled. "He broke Griff's heart? We need to pay him a visit."

"That was my plan." Zed gave him a frustrated look. "Griff says he doesn't love Luke. They were just fooling around... I don't know... kill him."

Noah made a face. "Repeat please."

"Griff says he doesn't love him, and that they were just fooling around. He says Luke is going to step up and co-parent with him, but they *aren't* in a relationship. I don't know if I believe him. If Luke fucks up, I'm going to kill him."

"I'll help, if you need me to. Everyone says Gramps knows a lot of places to bury people." Noah paused, disturbed. "They say that a lot actually. Maybe I should worry."

Zed laughed. "I think you're safe. Anyway, all that wasn't my real point."

Noah blinked. "There's more?"

"I'm mad as hell that Luke got my baby brother pregnant," Zed said, keeping his words clear and even. "I'm even angrier with myself because I'm jealous that Griff is having another kid."

"You want kids," Noah said thoughtfully.

Zed nodded and leaned forward. "I really do, and here I am not even dating anyone."

Noah felt sick to his stomach. "Any omega would be lucky to have you."

The frustration seemed to drain from Zed's face,

and he smirked. "You look like you're about to puke. Anyway, who said I wanted an omega?"

Zed moved closer, skirting around Peanut to stand in front of him. Noah knew the other man was huge, but when he was this close, Noah almost felt dainty.

"Oh, shit. I'm sorry. I know better than to assume." Noah flushed. He really didn't stand a chance with Zed if the man wasn't even gay. "I thought you were gay since Justin and Griff set you up with Sam –"

"Oh, I'm gay. I just have a thing for an alpha."

Noah's eyes grew wide. *Did he really say what I think he said?* "I'm an alpha."

Zed watched him, brown eyes full of heat. "Why don't you try some of your pickup lines on me?"

CHAPTER 8

Zed smirked as he watched Noah's eyes go wide.

He had suspected the younger alpha was attracted to him, but hearing Noah tell Jake that Zed made him happy cinched it. *Now, to convince him we fit.*

"How about it?" Zed asked, pushing in close to Noah.

"Can I have your picture?" Noah stuttered over his words, voice overly loud.

Zed cocked his head. "Okay?"

"I need to show Santa what I want for Christmas."

Zed laughed hard, body shaking. Once he could catch his breath, he grinned at Noah. "It is almost Christmas."

Noah flushed red and covered his eyes. "Did I really say that?"

Zed hooked his fingers in Noah's beltloops and pulled the man close. He waited until Noah looked up again. "I like your cheesy pickup lines when they're directed at me."

Noah licked his lips, and Zed couldn't resist. He leaned forward and pressed his mouth to Noah's. The younger alpha moaned, lips parting, and Zed didn't hesitate to deepen the kiss. Noah tasted better than Zed had imagined.

Noah's arms came around his waist and pulled Zed closer. Zed liked the feel of Noah's hands gripping his jacket. His dick was painfully hard in seconds.

Zed cupped the back of Noah's head and knocked his hat off. He threaded his fingers through Noah's hair.

They pulled apart for air, and Zed bit back a groan. Noah's lips were swollen, and his eyes were heavy with desire. Zed's fingers lightly massaged Noah's head, and the other alpha leaned into his touch.

"For weeks, we've spent every evening together," Zed said, trying not to let his emotions carry his words away. "I like spending time with you, Noah, and you're a good man. Can we give us a try?"

Noah gave him a worried look. "I didn't catch the first part."

Zed smiled softly and repeated himself.

Doubt filled Noah's face. "I'm a lot of work, Zed. I'm fortunate that I speechread well, but honestly, I only catch part of what people say most of the time. I have to piece together the rest through context. It's like fitting puzzle pieces together and hoping I can see the picture well enough to understand. By the time I do that, the conversation's moved on. That's with my family and friends doing everything they can to make it easier on me. It's frustrating having to wait on me."

"No, it isn't. You're *not* a lot of work." Zed stroked Noah's cheek. "Besides, I have all kinds of time and patience."

"I'm already attached to you," Noah whispered. "If we start something and you decide to leave, it's going to hurt."

"I won't leave unless you want me to." Zed made the sign for *pleasure*. "Being with you would be pure pleasure."

Noah gave him a half-smile. "You haven't seen me in the morning."

Zed kissed him again, lingering a little longer than he intended. "I'll show you how good we'll be together." He stepped back, pleased that Noah looked befuddled again. "I'm cooking dinner for you tonight."

Noah shook his head, eyes still a little dazed. "What was that?"

Zed smirked and signed his words. "I'm cooking dinner tonight."

Noah smiled slowly. "You really want me?"

"More than anything." It made him sad that Noah thought, even for a moment, that he was *too much trouble*.

"I don't know, Z. I'd rather have you as a friend, then not at all. What happens if you *do* get frustrated and leave?"

Never gonna happen, Zed thought and pushed back a sigh. "We don't have to rush. Let's just move slow and see how it goes. Okay?"

Noah gave him a doubtful look. "You won't leave?"

"I promise." Zed hadn't lied. He had time and patience enough to convince Noah that they would work. "We'll have dinner and talk, just like we do every night."

Zed pulled the stallmat from Peanut's stall and handed it to Noah to spray clean. They worked together quickly and ran through the final chores for the day while Zed pretended not to notice the shy looks Noah sent his way.

By the time the horses were fed and Peanut back in her stall, the storm had gotten worse. The short walk to the house, took quite a bit longer. The roar of the creek was muted by the snow, but the old waterwheel still turned.

Zed shivered and took off his outer gear in the mudroom. It was a familiar routine.

Noah's house was Zed's favorite place to be. The high ceilings and open spaces appealed to him. *It could use more plants*, he thought. The little aloe plant he'd given Noah looked lonely on the windowsill across from the kitchen.

It wasn't just the nice house that Zed liked. The company was the best part of each of Zed's days. Zed really had meant it when he'd told Noah he'd enjoyed their time together over the past few weeks.

Noah didn't mind that Zed was a bit of an overactive perfectionist. He just patiently waited while Zed took a while to clean stalls or sweep the barn as thoroughly as possible. He didn't complain when Zed washed the dishes by hand or fluffed the couch cushions after they spent the evening playing video games.

Noah smiled softly and handed Zed the mop so he could quickly clean the mudroom floor. *Yeah, he gets me.*

After cleaning up, Zed washed his hands and gathered a few things from the freezer and refrigerator. He was always surprised Noah had so much home canned and frozen vegetables, though he shouldn't be. He knew all about the Wilsons from Janelle and Abel.

He looked at Noah. "Do you like gumbo?"

Noah gave him a puzzled look, so Zed pulled the recipe up on his phone and showed it to him. "You have shrimp in the freezer. It'll be good."

Noah watched him, eyes bright with interest. "You like taking care of people."

Zed made sure he faced Noah as he started cutting vegetables. "I always have. Mom was… She wasn't mother material." Noah nodded his understanding, eyes focused on him. "I had to take care of Griff."

"Do you miss it?"

Zed smiled, nodding his head. "Yeah. Griff is grown up now and can take care of himself." He paused, hands stilling. "I meant to tell you that Griff and Bea are moving in with me."

"To save money for the new baby?"

Zed nodded again. "Luke is going to support them as much as possible, but Griff is stubborn." He made a face. He hated that he sometimes liked Luke. The damn alpha really cared about Griff, even if they didn't love each other.

Noah bit his lip, eyes narrowed in thought.

Zed didn't wait to be asked. He went ahead and repeated himself, taking a moment to sign *stubborn.*

Noah nodded. "The house has three bedrooms, so that will work in a pinch."

Zed resumed cutting the okra. "They have a cat that likes to chew on my plants."

Noah chuckled. "Uh oh. Eugenia and Maude are in trouble. At least you'll be able to coddle Griff like you want to."

"True." Zed grinned. "I love my honey bee too."

Noah's smile faded. "You really want to date me?"

Zed nodded. "When you're ready."

"If we do date," Noah said slowly, "will you tell Griff and Justin?"

"I can't keep it from them for long." Zed didn't like secrets. He never had. He'd keep this one for Noah only if he had to. "They keep trying to set me up on blind dates."

"Meddling and matchmaking could be a problem." Noah leaned back, shoulders tensed. "I don't want to have to show up on all your dates. People will start talking."

"Then I guess you better start soul searching, handsome. I'm more than ready to be yours." Zed put the pan of gumbo on the stove to cook. "Now, are you ready for Mario Cart?"

Noah cracked his knuckles. "Time to kick your ass."

~

A FEW HOURS LATER, THEY SAT ON THE COUCH, BELLIES full, and watched *Chopped*. *That's another thing about Noah,* Zed thought to himself. *He doesn't mind my obsession with cooking shows.*

Zed leaned forward, arms braced on his knees. "Damn it, don't overcrowd the deep fryer."

Noah watched him instead of the T.V., face full of amusement. "You're as bad as Reuben."

Zed smiled nervously. "Reuben likes *Chopped*?"

Noah's eyes narrowed. "Why does Reuben make you nervous?"

Zed leaned back and stretched an arm across the couch. "Nothing bad. I just admire him."

Noah smiled widely. "You have a crush on Reuben."

Zed flushed. "He cooks really well. He's creative and innovative while still keeping everything delicious."

"I only caught half of that, but you definitely have a bro crush." Noah laughed. "This is great. I'm texting Ernie in the morning."

Zed pulled Noah over his lap. The younger alpha was pure, solid, compact muscles and heavier than he'd thought.

Zed covered Noah's mouth with his own, cutting off the laughter. He sank into the kiss, savoring Noah's taste and the feel of his lips.

Noah moaned and grabbed Zed's shirt, tugging him close. His ass felt so damn good, grinding against Zed's hard dick.

He slid a hand over Noah's hip, then cupped the

other alpha's hard, covered dick. He traced the length. Zed couldn't decide if he wanted Noah's ass or dick first.

Noah grunted and arched into Zed's touch.

"Is this okay?" Zed asked, voice rough. He didn't want to hold back from Noah, and there were plenty of ways to show him they'd be good together.

"It's been a while." Noah wiggled around, eyes full of need. "Please."

Zed fumbled for a moment but managed to stand up with Noah in his arms. He strained a bit at his weight, but managed to make it as far as the stairs.

Noah watched him, heated eyes full of amusement. "Gonna try to carry me up the stairs, he-man?"

Zed snorted and set him down. "I'm trying to be romantic."

Noah cupped his face and kissed him, tongue swirling with Zed's. He leaned back. "I don't need to be swept off my feet. I need to be fucked into the mattress. Then I want you riding my dick."

Zed groaned and pulled Noah upstairs. He had yet to see the rest of Noah's house, and the upstairs was roomier than he expected. He saw five closed doors and a hall closet. "Which one is your room?"

Noah ran a hand over Zed's throat while he talked, then tugged him toward the first door on the left. "The others are three bedrooms and a bathroom."

The master bedroom was large and open. Noah didn't have much furniture in it, and Zed's eye twitched when he saw the unmade bed.

He forgot all about it when Noah grabbed a bottle

of lube from his nightstand and kissed Zed again. "I'm negative."

Zed struggled to form words. "Me too."

Noah helped him out of his clothes, eyes scanning Zed's bare skin. Zed knew he wasn't the most handsome man in the world – his ears were too big and his face too broad. The only thing he had going for him was his body.

Noah didn't seem to mind one bit. He traced his tongue over the tip of Zed's ear, then pressed small kisses all over his face.

Noah's hands smoothed over Zed's bare shoulders and over his chest. He leaned forward and licked first one nipple, then the other.

Zed tugged at Noah's clothes, wanting to see the other man. Where Zed was definitely imperfect, Noah was gorgeous. His light brown skin was smooth and warm, his muscles supple and firm. His beautiful round cheeks and gap-toothed smile made Zed's heart beat too fast.

Finally, Noah stood naked, and Zed took his time looking him over. He noted each freckle on his shoulders and his lean waist. He paid special attention to the long, hard dick standing to attention. *Yep, I want him in me*, he thought, licking his lips.

He pulled Noah to the bed and sat, pulling the other alpha on top of him.

Noah straddled him and pressed against him. Noah reached down and wrapped his calloused hands around their dicks, holding them together and stroking them.

Zed's head fell back, and he lost himself to Noah's touch. The heated pleasure increased with each stroke, and he knew he would come if they didn't slow down.

He lifted Noah and pressed him back on the bed. "Want to come inside you."

Zed started at his neck and slowly kissed his way down Noah's body. He kissed the alpha's broad chest and tight, pink nipples.

Noah's groans filled the air, and Zed smiled against his stomach. He liked the sound a little too well.

Noah hooked his arms under his legs, and Zed enjoyed the view for a moment. "Damn, that's a nice sight."

He stroked Noah's dick and slowly pressed a lubed finger into his hole. He took his time stretching him, then slowly slid inside, setting a steady rhythm.

Noah panted beneath him and watched Zed with heavy-lidded, heated eyes. Zed remembered his earlier words – *Fuck me into the mattress* – and increased his pace. He slammed into Noah's ass, shuddering as he tried to control himself.

"Don't hold back," Noah said, reading Zed too clearly.

Zed growled and let go. He pounded into Noah, lost in the heat and pleasure of the moment. Noah's moans grew louder, and he came hard, splattering against Zed's stomach. The heat of his cum was too much and set Zed off. He came, deep in Noah's ass, shuddering and falling against the other alpha.

Noah wrapped his arms around Zed and rolled

them over to their sides. "Damn, Zed. Why didn't we do that the day we met?"

Zed chuckled and cupped Noah's cheek. "I don't know."

"Stay the night?" Noah asked, voice sleepy.

"Of course." He pulled Noah close, their bodies fully entwined. There was nowhere he'd rather be.

A LOW MOAN WOKE ZED. HIS EYES OPENED, AND HE looked around Noah's bedroom, automatically checking for danger. It took him longer than it should have to notice Noah's body shaking in his arms.

"Fuck," he said, automatically keeping his voice low. The moonlight fell on Noah's pale, damp face.

"Please, no more," Noah muttered, fighting to break out of Zed's embrace. He let Noah go immediately, and Noah's breathing evened out.

Zed gently shook Noah's shoulder, and his eyes popped open. He looked around, frantic, body only settling when he saw Zed.

"I'm sorry. Did I wake you up?" Noah asked, voice rough from sleep.

Zed leaned over and turned the lamp on. He sat up and made the sign for *dream*. "You were dreaming."

Noah looked away. "I'm sorry."

Zed placed a finger under Noah's chin and turned him back to face him. "Please, talk to me."

Justin had told Zed that Noah's parents were assholes that had extorted money from the Wilson family for years. *That's not what's giving my man bad dreams.* Noah had mentioned a mental hospital when they first met. Zed hadn't pressed him then, but things were different now.

Noah swallowed hard. "I don't remember the attack that cost me my hearing. It was my first deployment, and I was only there for a week."

"A week?" Zed winced. "That's bad luck."

Noah nodded and smiled half-heartedly. "I joined the army to get away from my parents. Dad has a gambling problem, and Mom is a first-rate con artist. Life with them was unbearable, and they pulled me into everything they got into."

Zed frowned. "Why didn't you come here?"

Noah shrugged. "I didn't realize Elijah, Gramps, and Grammy would have taken me in. I had only visited them a handful of times. If I would have known, I would have come to Uncle Marco. I didn't know though. So, I joined the army. They couldn't reach me there."

Zed rubbed Noah's bare arms. He could see Noah as a soldier. He was young but had an assured way about him.

"After the attack, I was medically discharged." Noah blew out a breath. "The VA hospital wasn't as bad as I thought it would be. My doctor did what he could, but the damage was too much for even a cochlear implant." He pointed at his ear. "One of the nerve thingies they need doesn't work anymore."

"That had to be rough," Zed said thoughtfully. "Going from hearing to silence so quickly."

Noah nodded. "I'll always struggle with it. Elijah and the others… They help. It's not just that they try so hard to make things easier for me. They don't let me dwell on it. Now, it's just a part of me."

"Every part of you is beautiful." Zed barely kept himself from pulling Noah into a hug. He wanted to promise to always take care of Noah. To always be there to offer support. He didn't think Noah would believe it right now. *He'll see we're the real deal soon enough.*

"My parents came and picked me up from the hospital." Noah gave him a bitter look. "I thought they were worried about me. I needed help to adjust, and I thought that for once in my life, they were there to take care of me."

"The mental hospital?" Zed asked softly.

"They got one of their lawyer friends to declare me incompetent with the state. We left the VA hospital and went straight to St. Mercy's Psychiatric Hospital. They pushed through the psych evaluation needed, so my parents could start claiming my VA benefits on my behalf."

"What the fuck?" Horror filled Zed. He had known it was bad, but he hadn't realized it was that bad. "How is that possible?"

"Mom has a lot of shady connections." Noah's laugh was hoarse. "All that work for a modest monthly check."

"Noah," Zed whispered, giving in and pulling the alpha into his arms.

Noah shuddered, then wrapped his arms tightly

around Zed. "It was bad, Z. I fought back at first, so they drugged me and kept me strapped to a bed. It was… I could see what was happening around me. I just couldn't talk or move. My mind was all muddled."

Zed kissed Noah's head and stroked his back. *If those assholes show up here, I'll fucking kill them.*

"Then Elijah came." Noah leaned back, voice full of emotion. "I remember thinking he was just a dream at first. He brought Carter and some others, and they saved me. I remember Juan carrying me out of there, and I couldn't say anything."

Zed buried his face against Noah's neck, body trembling with anger. There was nothing he could do about any of it now, so anger wouldn't help anything. His body didn't care what his mind thought.

"Sometimes, I'll dream about being there again." Noah laughed harshly. "I don't dream about the attack, just that fucking horrible place. In my nightmares, no one knows where I'm at, so they can't come save me, and I can't move or talk. I can't save myself."

Zed leaned back. "That will never happen, Noah." He cupped Noah's face and made sure his man was watching him. "I'll always find you, no matter what. I have your back."

CHAPTER 9

*L*ater that week, Noah put his truck in park outside of Zed's house. The Wilsons had been called in to help Griff move, so instead of spending Sunday spoiling his horses with Jake's help, he had a load of boxes in the back of his truck.

Jake sat in the passenger seat. He smirked toward Noah. "Your man is here."

Noah cleared his throat, flushing slightly. "So he is. Did you get around to talking to your parents?"

It was Jake's turn to flush. "Yeah. They said they'll love me no matter what." He smirked again. "How much… set you up with Griff?"

Noah gave him a sour look. "I'm glad I only understood half of that."

Jake laughed, then jumped out of the truck.

Noah opened his door, stepped out, and looked around, noting who all had come to help get Griff and Bea settled. He saw Marco and Bennett, as well as most of their kids. Ray and Mateo were already moving furniture in, and Carter was with Doc Grover. Wait. *Carter* was with Doc Grover.

"Oh, shit." Noah hurried toward the two men. They looked far too pleased with themselves. "What did you two do?"

Noah's brother-in-law hugged him, then gave him an innocent look. "Whatever do you mean?"

"Griff already has a cat." Noah glared at Grover. "Zed has the sandwich club. They don't need more pets."

Carter shrugged. "It's not our fault Griff and Justin think Zed gave the miniatures to you. He's had more than one chance to build a barn."

"Carter." Noah growled after he pieced together what the man had said. "What did you do?"

"One of our neighbors moved away and left a cat behind. Justin said he knew just who to give it to."

Grover smiled widely. "I checked her over, and she's healthy. Olive is giving her to Zed now."

"Fuck." Noah ran toward the house, ignoring everyone and everything around him. It was a known fact that no one could tell Olive no. She was too damn cute.

He dodged passed Caden and Yeo and ran toward the kitchen. Zed would be guarding his plants from Griff's demon cat.

He pushed Justin out of the kitchen doorway and skidded to a stop when he saw them. *I'm too late.*

Olive looked up at Zed, her brown eyes huge and shimmery. She held up a fluffy, grey and white cat with a long, bushy tail.

Zed made a face but took the cat, letting Olive prompt him to hold it on its back like a baby. The cat lay passively in his arms, watching Zed with big grey eyes.

"Damn it." Noah turned around and glared at Justin. The man ran from the room, body shaking with laughter.

Griff moved closer to Noah. "It's just a cat, Noah." His eyes narrowed. "I see the way you look at my brother. Are you two dating?" He signed the word for *relationship*. "Wait, it's not really my business, is it?"

Noah smiled slowly, ignoring the dating question. "You're learning sign language for me?"

Griff flushed. "Zed is trying so hard, and it got me interested. I'm doing ASL, so I can help Zed practice."

Noah held his arms out. "You want a Wilson hug, don't you?"

Griff shook his head furiously. "No! Keep your Wilson hugs. Justin says that's how it all starts."

"Too late." Noah pulled him in and hugged him tightly.

Elijah and Grammy watched them curiously. They were sitting with Bea and the twins at the kitchen table. Snacks covered the surface, and Cooper's face was already covered in peanut butter.

Janelle gave him an amused look from where she stood on a ladder. A new fern hung in front of one of the wide windows. "He's been avoiding our hugs all day," she signed.

"You're ours now," Noah said, squeezing the omega.

Noah let Griff go and turned around when he felt

Olive's thin arms around his waist. He picked his niece up and hugged her too, spinning her around. He felt her small body shake with her giggles.

By the time he set her down, Griff had made his escape and hid behind Elijah. *Like he won't hug you,* Noah thought, shaking his head. Zed stared around the room, baffled, with a cat cradled in his arms.

Movement caught his eye, and Noah noticed Griff's cat, a sleek calico, jump onto the window sill to sniff at a row of succulents.

Noah rushed over, waving his arms. "Back, demon cat. Back!"

The cat looked at him, unimpressed, then pushed one of the small pots off the sill with its paw.

Noah winced and turned to Zed, giving him a sympathetic look.

Zed didn't seem concerned about the broken pot. He watched Noah and smiled that damn crooked smile of his. Noah barely noticed Griff hustling to the window to scoop up the cat while Grammy grabbed a broom to sweep up the mess.

He finally pulled his gaze away from Zed and noticed Gramps in the kitchen doorway. His grandfather's eyes watered as he looked between Noah and Zed.

Noah tilted his head, confused.

Gramps just smiled widely and signed, "I love you," before turning to grab a small box from Marco.

Noah shrugged and picked up the poor succulent. "I think we can repot it."

Zed bumped their shoulders together. "Yeah. Hold

this." He handed Noah the cat as if he was passing him a delicate infant.

Noah looked at the cat. "You better be nicer to the plants, furball."

The cat's intense stare was a little disconcerting.

A few hours later, Noah downed a bottle of water on the porch. Everything was moved in and most of it was unpacked. Wilsons were everywhere, and he needed a bit of peace.

He pulled his jacket close, blocking out the chilly wind. It was still snowing a bit, but it looked like the storm had finally passed. He startled when Marco sat beside him.

His uncle smiled and signed "I like Zed."

Noah tugged on the collar of his flannel shirt, then signed back. "I do too. He's a wonderful person."

Marco didn't say anything for a long moment, then signed, "How long have you been in love with him?"

Noah yelped. "What? I don't love him. We've been together one time. One time!"

"I'm happy for you, son." Marco paused and gave him a one-armed hug, then leaned back again. "I see the way you look at him. You'll figure it out soon enough, but it's okay to take your time."

"He's an alpha."

Marco blinked. "So?"

"He's not an omega." Noah bit his lip.

Marco looked baffled. "What's your point?"

"We can't have kids."

"You've been together *one time*, Noah," Marco repeated, adding emphasis to his signs before grinning.

"Besides, there is more than one way to have children. *If* you even want to have children. We just want you to be happy. How you get there is up to you."

Noah leaned his head back. "I knew you would say that."

Marco arched a brow. "Then why are you afraid?"

Noah gave him an uncertain look. "What if he gets tired of dealing with me?"

"Then he isn't the man we think he is," Marco said. "I have a shovel, and Dad knows all the best places in the woods. Grammy will drive."

Noah shook his head. "That shouldn't make me feel better. Does Gramps have a lot of buried bodies out in the woods?"

Marco hugged him again before leaning back. "You need to trust your heart, Noah. Sometimes you overthink things." He tilted his head. "Take your time, but give him a chance."

"You didn't answer my question about Gramps."

"I'm not stupid." Marco grinned. "I don't think Zed will end up in the woods."

Noah smiled. "He's special, Uncle Marco. He's like this larger-than-life, fussy mama bear. He loves taking care of everyone around him. I like being able to take care of him too. When we're together, it's easy and calm, except when it's sexy and hot."

Marco laughed. "I understand."

"I just really don't want to lose him," Noah finished, sighing. "I'd rather just be his friend, then lose him altogether."

Marco shook his head. "If you care about him, be

brave enough to be with him. Otherwise, you'll have to watch someone else step up and take your place."

Noah growled. "I don't like that idea."

Marco patted his knee. "Good. Let's go in and grab lunch. Bennett made your favorite chicken salad."

They stood and Noah hugged his uncle. "Thank you."

Marco squeezed him tight. "I love you, Noah. When you decide Zed is yours, let us know, alright?"

"I will."

A few moments later, Noah grabbed a plate of food and sat beside Zed. His alpha laughed with Janelle about something, then turned, making sure Noah could see his face as they spoke.

Noah hid a smile. *It's not a big deal. Really. I'm not falling in love with him.*

Elijah pushed in on Noah's other side and watched him with hearts in his eyes. *Shit, my face is giving all my insides away.* It wouldn't be long until all of Noah's family knew he cared about Zed.

Noah settled his head on Elijah's shoulder, breathing in his familiar smell. Elijah was safety and love. He always would be.

One day, Zed's scent will be as familiar to me as Elijah's, he thought. Noah didn't know if that excited him or scared him.

LATER THAT NIGHT, NOAH SAT IN ONE OF THE overstuffed leather chairs in his living room with Bea and a book in his lap while Olive and Zed played Candy Land on the floor in front of the television. The twins sat near his chair, coloring.

A couple of Zed's potted plants sat on his windowsill, and Maude and Eugenia hung in front of the largest window in the room. The fluffy, grey and white cat, Tuffy, lay across the back of his couch, sleeping. The cat had zero interest in potted plants. The only things she seemed to like to do were eat, nap, and love on either Noah or Zed.

Bea tapped his arm and pointed at the page.

Noah cleared his throat and went back to reading the kid's book in front of him. Olive and the twins often stayed the night with him, but having Zed and Bea there made things even better.

His phone vibrated in his pocket, and he pulled it out, smiling at the text message.

Elijah: The house is QUIET! Enjoy being the best uncle in the world. I'm stalking my alpha for a little fun of our own.

Noah chuckled, then set the phone on the side table next to the chair. Time to read a little girl her bedtime story.

CHAPTER 10

A week later, the humming vibration of Noah's phone woke Zed. So far, he'd spent every night at Noah's house. It wasn't that he didn't like living with Griff and Bea. He loved them both. It was more that he couldn't get enough of his sweet alpha.

Griff thought it was the most entertaining thing he'd ever seen but had agreed to hold off on telling Justin until Zed and Noah were a little more settled.

He yawned and looked around the room before sitting up to grab Noah's pants from the floor.

He pulled the cellphone out, then cursed when he saw a partial text on the screen. *You stupid son of a –*

Noah mumbled something and curled against him. Zed hated to wake him up but knew this was important. He shook Noah's shoulder.

Noah blinked a few times, then smiled sweetly. "Hey."

Zed kissed him, then handed him the phone. "I think your dad texted you."

All the sleepy happiness drained from Noah's eyes, and he sat up quickly, unlocking his phone. Zed looked over his shoulder.

You stupid son of a bitch! After everything I've done for you, how could you do this to me? I needed that money. Send me five thousand dollars by TOMORROW, or you'll regret the day you were born. That dirty omega whore may be useless, but I know Dad gave you money. I swear if you try anything, I'll come to Hobson Hills and burn that pretty little ranch of yours to the ground.

Noah paled. "He'll do it. Shit, I don't have five thousand dollars lying around. I put everything I get into the ranch, even what Gramps gave me. Horses are expensive, especially the rescue horses, and I'm hiring a full-time ranch hand soon."

Zed shook his head. "You're not giving that bastard anything. We'll call the sheriff, and you'll get a new restraining order."

Noah's hands shook, and he looked confused. "Restraining order. I can do that. At least he's not targeting Elijah."

Noah's phone buzzed again, and he winced before looking at the screen. Zed leaned over and read the text.

Ray: Juan's dad passed last night. He needs us.

Noah looked up, dazed. "Fuck, I need to go to Arizona. Juan needs me, and he's always been there for me. I need to be there for him. What am I going to do? Damn it."

Zed leaned in and kissed him. "I'll call the sheriff

while you pack. I'll stay here while you're gone and keep an eye on the ranch."

Noah shook his head. "Can you repeat the second part?"

Zed smiled softly. "I'll stay here while you're gone. I won't let anything happen to your ranch."

Noah gave him a pained look. "You won't forget me while I'm gone?"

He laughed. "That's impossible."

"We should be exploring this," Noah said, waving a hand between them. "I shouldn't run off so soon after —"

"You're not running off, Noah. You need to help a friend." Zed sat up and reached for his own cell phone. This was what Zed was *good* at, and he couldn't help but be a little happy to have the chance to show Noah he could be useful. "You can count on me. This is what being in a relationship is about."

Noah nodded, face full of uncertainty. "I'll call Dean and ask him to do the chores and help Diane with the appointments for the next few days. Doc is coming by to look at Otis's teeth."

Zed leaned forward and kissed him. "We'll take care of it."

He would protect Noah's home and the horses, and damn, he hoped Steven fucking Wilson decided to show up. He'd love to have a talk with the fucker.

ZED LAUGHED AND SNAPPED A PICTURE TO SEND NOAH.

Noah's cousin Tali and Jake were pampering Carrot while Noah was gone. The two were each kissing one of the horse's cheeks. The poor horse missed Noah, and Zed's man had only been gone a day.

You're not the only one, Carrot. Zed should have slept just fine without Noah by his side, but that wasn't the case.

Tuffy meowed softly from Butter's back. The miniature gelding was the most placid of the Sandwich club, and Tuffy had taken a liking to him. She curled up on his back, yawning wide before settling into a nap. The cat didn't even seem to mind the red Christmas sweater Ernie had knitted for her.

Zed took a quick picture of them and sent it to Noah too.

"Back to work." Zed quickly went back to feeding the horses while Jake and Tali laughed and joked as they brushed them down. Carrot and the three miniatures strolled behind him in the hallway. Each time he stopped, they'd take a minute to say hello to the horse he fed.

"I can't wait for Papa to see you with the sandwich club." Jake snickered. "Even Noah doesn't let them all follow him around."

Diane and Dean were with a new patient in the other barn, and Zed was glad it was Dean and not him. The patient had wrinkled her nose as soon as she set foot in the barn and complained about the smell.

Tali shot him looks as she braided a red ribbon through Jelly's black mane. "You and Noah, huh?"

"How did you know that?" Zed gave her a curious

look. He wasn't trying to hide his feelings for Noah, but he hadn't thought they were being obvious.

Tali gave him a flat look. "I've seen the way you talk about him. I can only imagine how adorkable you two are together."

"They're horrible," Jake said, laughing. "Noah gets all flirty, and you *do not* want to hear his pickup lines. Then Zed here gets all gooey and overprotective."

Zed grinned. "Yeah. That's us."

"Well, isn't that interesting?" Gramps said from behind him.

Zed spun around, almost dropping the cannister of feed he carried. "Uh, hello, sir." *How the hell did he get in here without me hearing?*

Noah's grandfather leaned against an empty stall. Peanut pranced over and whinnied, demanding the man give her the attention she deserved. Gramps gave her some pats, then turned back to him.

The older man's eyes sparkled, but he kept his face stern. "I hear you're messing around with my grandson. You and me should have a little talk."

Tali snickered and pulled Jake with her toward the door. "We'll work on feeding in the other barn."

Zed stood straight. He had nothing to be ashamed of, and he'd served under scarier men. *I was a Marine, damn it!* Gramps narrowed his eyes, and Zed seriously thought of running for the door. The thought of Noah's smile and laugh kept him steady. *Being with Noah is worth a little awkward conversation.*

"You know my Noah is a very special person,

right?" Gramps asked, expression making it clear that there was only one correct answer.

"Yes, sir," Zed said, getting the sudden urge to salute. "He's a good man, and I would be lucky to have him."

Jelly pressed against his side, almost knocking him over. He patted her back and checked to make sure Butter and Carrot weren't trying to eat the other horses' food. They were nosing around Snickerdoodle's stall.

Gramps chuckled and patted Peanut again. "Relax, son. You don't have to worry about me. If Noah wants you, then I'm happy. All you have to do is treat him well. I know Justin and Griff pretty well now, and they think the world of you."

Zed let some of the tension drain from his shoulders. "I care a lot about Noah. I'll do my best by him."

Gramps patted his back. "Good. Now, I really came by to help out since Noah's with Juan. What can I do?"

"If you can finish feeding them, I'll put the motion sensors I bought up. The horses' diets are on the card pinned to the stall."

"Motion sensors?" Gramps gave him a worried look. "Please tell me you're just being an overprotective former Marine."

Zed rubbed his hands through his short hair. "I really wish Noah was here to tell you this."

"Just spit it out, son." Gramps stroked Peanut's ears. "I can handle it."

"Steven texted Noah right before he left. He

threatened to burn down the stables if Noah didn't send him money."

"Damn it." Gramps squeezed his eyes shut. "Where did I go wrong with that boy? He's been a greedy, self-centered, little shit since he could walk."

Zed leaned against the stall beside him. "The only person responsible for Steven Wilson's behavior is Steven Wilson. Sometimes people are just shit."

Gramps opened his eyes and gave Zed a sad look. "Sometimes good kids are born from shit people too."

Zed flushed. "You're talking about my dad, right?"

Gramps nodded. "You and me have a lot in common. I think we both need to remember that blood is one part of a body. I didn't realize Stevie was as bad as he was until he was in high school. He has a way of making you see what you want to see. I gave him every chance I could, but I won't let him hurt my family."

Zed chewed on his lip for a moment. "I worry sometimes that I'll be like *him*. Griff is kind and giving, but I can be hard sometimes. I don't want to hurt Noah the way Joshua Ames hurt my mom." He couldn't bring himself to call him *dad* right then.

"I think you worrying about it makes you different," Gramps said, giving him a kind look. "Then there's the way you care for Griff, Justin, and your nieces. You're a decent person, Zed. I don't see you abandoning a family or two because things get hard."

Snickerdoodle whinnied and stomped her foot.

Zed laughed. "I think she wants her breakfast."

"On it." Gramps went to the back and started putting together the horse's breakfast.

Zed breathed a sigh of relief. Gramps Wilson was a good guy, so Zed really didn't understand why he was so nervous about being around him. *Probably because Noah loves him so much.*

"How do you like working at Abel's place?" Gramps asked from the first stall.

"I like it quite a bit actually."

"Why do you sound so surprised?" Gramps gave him a curious look.

"Gardening has always been a hobby, but I never tried farming." Zed shrugged. "Hell, I was a sniper. It feels strange going from a combat career to farming and brewing. I knew almost nothing about it." He smiled softly and patted Snickerdoodle's neck. The Palomino was a bit standoffish until she got to know you. "Abel and Janelle have been real patient with me."

Fortunately, the brewery was only open a couple of days a week in December. The hard work happened the rest of the year.

Gramps chuckled. "Abel says you're a godsend. He's a hard worker, but running all that while growing a daughter gets challenging. Janelle likes you too. She said you have a way with plants."

Zed grinned. "Janelle's my hero."

"Really?" Gramps snorted. "Of all my grandkids, I worry about her the most."

"You shouldn't." Zed went to the back, Jelly following him, and gathered the sensors he had bought and the tools he needed. "She reminds me of a honeybee, flitting from flower to flower and leaving behind something special in each place."

Gramps blinked, mouth hanging open. "Explain."

"She has the part-time job at the library where she gets to help people find information, entertainment, whatever they need, but that's not enough. She goes to Abel's and gets him situated and sitting pretty with his hops, then she goes to Farm Fresh and sells her greenhouse plants which bring the store a nice little income in the spring." Zed laughed. "She's always spreading her affection through her plants. She gave me Maude, and Noah says she's always sneaking over and planting things in the fall and spring. She's never still, but she's always there."

Gramps smiled slowly. "Well, I didn't think of it like that. I worry because she doesn't seem to want to settle."

Zed shrugged, starting to understand why Jake had been worried about what his parents would think of him not wanting a relationship. "Does she really need to be married with three kids to be settled? She's happy how she is."

Gramps snorted. "Damn it, why do you have to make sense?"

The barn door opened, and Tali led their new patient inside. "Here they are, Jenna. Jelly's my favorite."

Noah's newest patient wiped her eyes. "Oh my god, I didn't think anything could be cuter than Jasmine, but look at them."

The three miniatures knew exactly who she was talking about. Jelly left Zed's side and went straight to Tali, and Peanut was quick to follow her. Tali started walking Jenna through how to groom the two miniatures.

Diane shut the barn door behind them and sidled over to stand next to Zed. "This was just what Jenna needed. Do you mind her playing with your horses? Tali really wanted her to see them."

"I don't mind at all," Zed said, shaking his head. "I'm glad they're helping."

Diane smiled as she watched Jenna and Tali. "Horses can be the most gentle and honest animals. Jenna needs some of that in her life." She turned to him. "Jake said to tell you Dean and him will handle the other barn. He seemed concerned Gramps over there was going to try to neuter you."

Gramps laughed and patted Zed's shoulder. "That's only if he hurts my grandson."

Zed winced. "I'm getting away from you both. I think I prefer the snow to this topic."

THE NEXT EVENING, JANELLE LINED UP SIX MORE SMALL potted succulents on one of Noah's windowsills. "You should bring all your plants over. They would like it here."

Zed looked up from the page in the coloring book he was helping Bea fill in. "I really should. Griff's cat hates them."

"Dobby kitty soft and gives hugs," Bea said, picking up a green crayon. "Loves him."

Janelle gave Zed a knowing look. "I can see why you didn't ask Griff to rehome him."

Zed chuckled. "I couldn't have done that anyway. Griff loves the cat. He loves that house too. It suits him."

Janelle smirked. "You know the house comes with your job, no matter if you live in it or not. Maybe you should bring more of your stuff over here. Noah won't mind a roommate."

"Don't give me ideas," Zed muttered, coloring the flower a light pink. He missed Noah too much, and he had just been gone two days.

Bea laughed and colored over his flower with her crayon.

"You're rotten." His phone beeped loudly, and he stood quickly, grabbing it from the coffee table. He opened the app linked to his sensors.

"Shit. Something big is at the door to the rescue horse barn." He looked up. "Will you watch Bea?"

"Yeah." Janelle nodded. "I'm calling Sheriff McKenzie too. There shouldn't be anything that big out there right now."

Zed hurried to the mudroom and pulled his boots and coat on. He ran out the backdoor and almost fell on his ass when he slid across the bridge. It was covered with ice. *Need to put better rails on this thing.*

He saw the man through the falling snow. The outside lights were motion activated, so he was fully visible.

The man poured something from a fuel jug in front of the barn door.

Zed growled and barreled into the man, turning him around and punching his jaw. The man fell back, landing on his ass, and the gas jug went flying.

"Who the hell are you?" the man asked, holding a hand to his face. How he could possibly look offended right then, Zed didn't understand.

"I know who you are, asshole." Zed snarled. Steven Wilson shared his features with his sons, but they were surface similarities. Zed could see the petulant mouth and cruel eyes.

"Get out of here before I call the police." Steven struggled to his feet. "This is my son's ranch."

"The son that was just granted a restraining order against you." Zed pulled him up, body trembling. He badly wanted to hit the man again and to put his full strength behind it.

Steven smiled, face lighting up with charm. "You're misinformed. My son and I argue sometimes, but he knows I'm here."

Flashing blue lights cut through the snow, and Steven paled and started to struggle. "Let me go."

Zed smiled. "I think we'll just wait right here. Trust me, the other option isn't pleasant for you."

The police cruiser came to a stop next to them, and Tanner and Sheriff McKenzie both got out of the car, hands on their guns.

"You got here fast," Zed said, eyes trained on the wiggling man he had by the throat.

"We've been patrolling nearby since Mr. Wilson here made his threats," Tanner said, smiling amiably.

"Zed, why don't you let the man go, so we can take it from here."

Zed scowled. "I don't want to."

Sheriff McKenzie patted his back. "I don't blame you, but we need you to fetch the video feed from the security cameras."

"Someone needs to collect that gasoline can too." Tanner stood behind Steven and pulled his arms behind him. He started reading him his rights.

"I've done nothing wrong," Steven protested. "I'm just here visiting my son."

"You know there's a restraining order against you, Mr. Wilson." Sheriff McKenzie gave the man a flat look. "The papers were delivered yesterday, and I imagine they prompted this visit."

Steven curled his lip. "Obviously Noah isn't here, so it shouldn't matter."

"You were ordered to stay off the ranch," Sheriff McKenzie said, then turned his back on the man. "I'll take care of the gas, if you'll go ahead and get that footage, Ames."

Zed released Steven's throat and walked away with the sheriff. "Sorry about that."

"You managed not to kill him, so I think that's progress."

Zed snorted. "I really wanted to."

Sheriff McKenzie winced. "Can you please not tell me things like that?"

Zed laughed, then went to the back of the barn for the security camera footage. Most of the horses were still sleeping, but Peanut nickered as he passed. He stopped to hug her and buried his face into her mane.

"I wanted to kill him, Peanut." She whinnied softly, and Zed felt some of the tension drain away. "Okay. I'm going to get the footage."

A few hours later, Zed cuddled Bea in his lap. Gramps and several other Wilsons were wandering about the house. They were shaken up about Steven's reappearance.

"I'm staying here until he's charged," Abel said, glaring over his huge pregnant belly. "I'll kill the asshole if he tries to hurt Noah again. Plus, I can't lose Zed. He's my right hand man, damn it."

Zed arched a brow. He kind of wanted to see Abel take on Steven Wilson. He had no doubt the pregnant omega would kick the alpha's ass in a glorious fashion.

"Calm down, mi alma," Mateo said, rubbing his fiancé's back. "You don't need to jump into danger. I'll stay here instead. We'll keep an eye on things."

"Fuck that, I'm staying." Janelle growled and paced the floor. "Noah is my favorite cousin."

"Hey now," Harper, another of Noah's cousins, said. "There's like a thousand cousins here, Janelle, so be nice. Besides, I'm a good shot. I'll stay here."

A young beta Zed hadn't met yet tapped a pencil against his chin. "We could set traps and create a patrol schedule."

"Traps? He's not Bigfoot, Shawn. You sound as bad as Ernie." Zoe, another cousin, rolled her eyes.

How many fucking cousins does Noah have? Zed looked around. *Too many.*

The door to the mudroom slammed open, and two large alphas stormed into the room. Zed recognized them from around the stables.

"Dean told us Noah's dickhead father tried to burn the stables down," one of the men said. "Where is the fucker? Saul and I will handle him."

"Hi, Emmet," Shawn said. "I'll just put you and Saul on the patrol schedule."

Dean nodded grimly. "All hours of the day, Shawn."

Zed shifted in his seat. He had known Noah had a large family and plenty of friends, but the reality was a little daunting. He wanted to be the one to take care of Noah, damn it.

"I'm concerned about Rachael's whereabouts," Noah's Aunt Anna said. "She's usually hip deep in trouble, right alongside Steven."

"I'll text Ray and have him look into it," Dean said, pulling out his phone.

"Wait, Dean," Marco said. "Juan needs them all right now. Let's hold off until they get home. The sheriff said he could at least keep Steven for a few days before he posts bail."

"We'll keep eyes on him after he gets out," Zoe said, face grim. "We need to keep Noah safe. He's gone through too much to have to deal with that dickhead now."

Zed pushed everything away and closed his eyes. He knew Noah would be safe because he would be right here with him.

Someone nudged his shoulder, and Zed looked to his right. Elijah sat beside him on the couch, Connor on his lap. Zed smiled. Noah's brother was one of Zed's favorite people. He didn't know him well, but he didn't have to. *Elijah saved Noah.*

"You'll be here, won't you?" Elijah asked, whispering. "You're in love with Noah."

Zed's mouth dropped open. "I'm not –" He thought for a moment. "Holy shit, I'm in love with him."

He adored Noah's calm and steady personality, the way he pampered his horses, the way he cared so deeply for his family and friends, the gap-toothed smile, and the way Noah completely gave himself to Zed. All of it was too much to resist.

Elijah giggled. "That's how it happens in the Wilson family." He turned serious. "Don't worry. I won't say anything. You all haven't been together long, and to be honest, you're going to have to show Noah that you two will work. He wants to be with you so much, but he's scared. Our parents made sure he didn't think he was worth much growing up."

Zed blinked, brain still stuck on the fact that he loved Noah. "What do I do?"

Elijah gave him a sly look. "We all want Noah to have more protection since our dad has decided to focus all his jerkiness on him."

"I'm staying right here with him," Zed said, scowling. "I'll protect him."

Elijah's smile was far too smug. "Exactly."

CHAPTER 11

A few days later, Noah struggled to keep his eyes open in the backseat of Ray's Jeep. Dealing with strangers was exhausting. Hell, dealing with groups of people, whether he knew them or not, was exhausting.

They were an hour away from Hobson Hills, and there was a new snowstorm coming in. He kind of missed the warmer weather in Arizona.

He didn't pay any attention to the conversation happening around him. Ernie leaned his head on Noah's shoulder and slept, but Ray and Carter were talking up front.

Noah leaned his head against Ernie's. He still wasn't exactly sure how he had managed to become part of this pack. When Carter and Elijah came to save him, Carter had taken Noah under his wing. Along with Carter came Juan and Ray and, somehow, Ernie too.

He thought about Juan. He hated that his friend was going through so much right then. His dad had passed away, and someone had surprised him with a mini Juan at his dad's wake. Despite what the surprise woman had said, Noah didn't believe for one moment that Juan had known about the child and abandoned him. If Juan had known about Oscar, Noah's friend would have taken him in right away.

Juan's too good a person for that. Just like Zed. Noah's eyes fluttered shut, and he smiled as he thought about Zed. His alpha had sent him pictures of the horses every day. Jake and Dean had enlisted Tali to help with the chores while he was gone, and they were going overboard with the pampering. Every horse in the stables *really* didn't need hair bows and daily massages.

Noah fell asleep with a smile on his face.

"Damn it, Noah, I want kids," Zed said, frustrated. "The sex is okay, but you and me can't be a real family."

Noah shook his head, heart beating fast. "We can adopt kids or hire a surrogate. We can be a family. I promise."

He reached out to touch Zed's arm, but the other alpha shook him off. "Fine." Zed scowled. "You want to know the truth? I'm tired of this. Every day with you exhausts me, Noah. I've tried. I really have, but you're not enough for me. You're too clingy and too much work. Can you imagine how much harder it would be if we did have kids? They'd have to deal with you too."

Noah felt his body shake with his sobs. "Please, don't go, Z. I love you."

Zed shrugged. "That's your problem."

He woke in a panic, body jerking. "Zed, don't leave!"

Noah panted and took in the darkened interior of Ray's Jeep and the flickering lights of the gas station they were parked at. He slowly caught his breath, absently noting the front seat was empty. Movement caught his eye and he looked to the side.

Ernie watched Noah with wide eyes.

"Shit." Noah groaned.

Ernie slid closer and hugged Noah's arm. "Do you need to talk?" Noah could barely read his lips in the dim light.

Noah shook his head. "I'm okay. It was just a bad dream."

"You like Zed?"

Noah gave him a shaky smile. "Zed's a nice guy, but we're just friends."

The lie felt heavy on his tongue. Noah had fallen for the man over the past couple of months. There was no getting around that fact, even though it scared the shit out of him.

Ernie arched a brow. "Really?"

Noah shrugged. "That's how it has to be."

They didn't have time to talk more because Ray and Carter came back to the car, faces grim. Ray opened Noah's door and signed. "There was an incident while we were gone."

Carter got into his seat and turned around to face Noah. "Your dad showed up at your ranch."

Noah's body jerked. "No. Did he hurt someone? Are Zed and Elijah alright?"

Ray settled a hand on his knee, drawing his attention. "Everyone is alright. Zed stopped him from damaging your ranch. He spent a couple of nights in jail before posting bond. He'll be charged with…"

Noah couldn't follow the rest of Ray's explanation. It was too dark to see well, but he could figure out his dad would be back in court soon.

Zed will probably run for the hills as soon as I get home, Noah thought, heart heavy. The other alpha would wait until Noah was there to take care of the horses, but there was no way he'd want to try anything with Noah now. *It's probably for the best.*

Ray tilted Noah's face up to meet his kind eyes. "I'll do some digging. The more information you have, the better." He hugged Noah, then leaned back. "It'll be alright. We won't let that bastard hurt you again."

Noah scowled. "I can take care of myself."

Carter nodded. "You can, but why should you have to do this alone?"

Ernie shuffled in his seat and slipped his arms around him. Noah couldn't stifle the warm feeling spreading through him. He hadn't been alone since the day Elijah and the others had rescued him. Why should he be now?

When Zed left, it would hurt. There was no getting around that. Noah leaned back into Ernie's embrace. He wouldn't be alone, though, and that was something. He just wished he'd never hoped for more.

They were back on the road soon. Ray dropped Ernie off, then drove past Carter and Elijah's house.

Noah gave him a confused look. "You forgot Carter."

Carter turned around and said something, but Noah couldn't see his face well enough in the dark interior of the car.

"Sorry, I can't see your lips."

Carter reached back and patted Noah's leg before turning back around.

Ray parked the Jeep in front of Noah's house, and they all piled out. He didn't get far before the door slammed open and Elijah and Olive ran for him. Elijah grabbed Carter's arm and pulled him to Noah so he could hug them both.

Noah ruffled Olive's hair and hugged her and Elijah.

Movement at the door caught his eye. Zed stood in the door, Bea perched on a hip and Dean's son Min on the other. Elijah's twins stood on either side of him.

Noah looked away. *He'll be a good dad one day. Whatever fucking omega he ends up with had best know how lucky he is.*

When Elijah finally let them go, Olive tugged Noah toward the house.

Zed tilted his head, watching Noah curiously, but stepped out of the way so they could all go inside. Noah jumped when he noticed Ray behind him. He'd assumed his friend had headed home already.

Noah came to a stop when he started past the kitchen, finally noticing his surroundings. Plants were everywhere. Everywhere. *Did he bring all his plants here?*

There were also cookbooks on a shelf in his kitchen, right alongside Noah's framed pictures of his family. He squinted. It looked like there were new additions there too – a couple of pictures of Justin, Tanner, and their newborn Rhonda, several of Griff and Bea, and a few of Griff and Zed when they were kids. There was even a picture of Zed with several other Marines.

Noah picked up one of a much younger Zed. He looked to be around ten or so. His big ears and solemn expression made him easy to recognize.

Olive pulled him away from the kitchen and into the living room. A new bookshelf sat next to the television. Games and children's books lined the lower shelves, and mysteries, gardening books, and more cookbooks filled the top.

A Christmas tree sat in front of one of the windows, completely decorated with presents underneath. Noah recognized touches of Olive and the twins in the tree's decorations, but a sloppily painted ornament reminded him a lot of Bea.

Noah ran a hand through his hair, dislodging his hat. Zed was supposed to be running for the hills, not settling in for a long stay.

Olive tugged on his hand. She had that puppy dog look on her face, and her eyes were steadily getting brighter. "Mr. Z is going to stay with you so you'll be safe. That's okay, right?"

"Yeah." Noah's throat felt thick, and he finally met Zed's gaze. The other alpha didn't look impatient or annoyed. He looked as solid and calm as he always did.

Ray set Noah's bags down and reached for Min. The little boy's face lit up when he saw Ray, and he held his arms out for his dad.

"Were you visiting your friend?" Ray asked Min.

Noah had no idea what the little boy said, but he had gotten a lot of pictures of Bea and Min playing the last few days. It looked like the two toddlers got along well.

Ray patted his shoulder. "I'll call you if I find anything on Steven or Rachel. Let me know if you need me, Noah."

"Thanks, Ray."

Elijah hugged him again. "You look exhausted. I'll come by in the morning, and Zed and I will bake you some apple muffins."

Carter grinned and slung Cooper over one shoulder and Connor the other. "I think we'll come by too, right, Olive?"

She nodded. "I love apple muffins."

"You love apple everything, just like your daddy," Noah said, smiling. "I'll see you all in the morning."

He watched them leave from the front window, then noticed shadows moving outside. Someone was leaning against the rescue barn door.

Noah growled. "Someone's outside."

Zed settled a hand on his shoulder, and Noah turned to watch him. "That's just Emmet. He's on schedule tonight."

"Schedule? Did I understand that right?"

Zed grinned. "Your cousins are something special. Shawn put together a schedule so that two people are constantly watching the ranch. It's Emmet and Saul's turn right now."

"Seriously? Dad is just one person, and I'm not helpless." Noah looked down. "I'm sorry, Zed. I shouldn't have dragged you into this."

Zed set Bea on the floor and pulled Noah into his

arms. He made sure Noah was watching him before speaking. "Everyone wants to do this for you. We know you're strong. Hell, look at everything you've done the past few years."

"What about Elijah?" Noah asked. "I know Dad seems like he's focusing on me, but he knows I love Elijah."

Zed nodded. "I know someone's been staying with him while Carter was gone. I'll have Shawn put his house on the schedule too."

Noah snorted. "The schedule. Fuck, my family is way too protective. It's too cold outside for a sane person to want to sneak around."

Zed buried his face against Noah's neck, making him shiver.

He leaned into Zed's arms and absently looked around the room again. "You've moved in."

Zed pulled back and gave him a wary look. "It seemed like a good idea at the time, but I can pack my stuff up and –"

"No!" Noah shook his head. "No, it's great. I want you here as long as you want to be here."

Zed licked his lips. "I want to be here with you. I don't know if your dad will come back or not, but…"

Noah winced. "Can you repeat the last part?"

Zed smiled softly and cupped his cheek. "I want to be here if you need me."

Noah closed his eyes and pressed his face against Zed's hand. He wanted Zed to want to be with him because he loved him. *Take what you can get*, he reminded himself. "Thank you."

When he opened his eyes again, he noticed Tuffy padding down the stairs. The fluffy cat wound around his ankles, and Noah bent and petted the cat before she decided to nap on the back of the couch.

"You also have a cat now," Zed said, nodding at Tuffy. "She's yours, not mine, and no take backs."

Noah chuckled. "That just means that Justin and Griff will try to get you another pet."

Zed laughed, and Noah enjoyed the vibrations from Zed's body. "Griff is too busy enjoying taking over the house. He was happy to help me move. I think he may have gotten tired of me trying to force feed him every morning."

Noah frowned. "He's eating well, yeah?"

Zed sighed. "He works too hard. He's wants to get in as many hours as he can before he has to go on paternity leave."

"Are you sure you want to leave him?" Noah asked, swallowing hard. He didn't want to give Zed an out, but Griff could use some pampering right now."

Zed smiled. "I'm sure. Justin and his alpha are helping me pester Griff into taking care of himself."

Noah watched Bea settle down on the floor with her coloring books. "I'll help too."

Zed's kiss took Noah by surprise. The sweetness turned hot quickly, and Noah was reminded of how much he'd missed Zed over the past week.

"I THINK YOU TWO WOULD MAKE A GOOD COUPLE,"

Justin said, grinning. The Wilson family Christmas party was in full swing, and Noah had never felt so hunted. Justin had been after him the second he walked in the door. "You and Griff make so much sense, Noah. Think about it. You're already friends, and you're both single. Just go on one date. That's all."

"I have to piss." He turned and ran toward the kitchen. Reuben arched a brow when Noah ran past him, grabbed a sugar cookie, then crawled under the small kitchen table.

He saw Justin's feet walk in the door, but the omega didn't stay long. He stepped closer to Reuben, then turned and left.

Reuben waited a few minutes, then crouched down in front of him. "What's going on?" he signed. Noah thought it was interesting that Ernie's husband preferred signing to speaking, but he appreciated it, especially on days like this. He was exhausted already.

"I can't tell him I don't want to date Griff. I might hurt their feelings." Noah *really* didn't want to make Justin and Griff mad.

Reuben shook his head and handed Noah a plate of snacks before he stood back up.

The kitchen door opened again, and Noah recognized Olive's brown fuzzy boots. A few moments later, his niece crawled under the table with him, and they worked on the plate of food. Olive didn't bother asking why he was under the table; she just leaned against him and signed her thoughts.

"I wished for a horse for Christmas," Olive said. Elijah's family typically opened presents with Noah *after* the annual Wilson party, so they could spend Christmas morning with Carter's parents.

Noah winced. "Did you tell Carter that?"

Olive's smile was full of mischief. "Of course. I know Dad got me one because they wouldn't let me in the barn yesterday. I wonder if it'll be a little one like the sandwich club, or if it'll be big like Stinkbug and Carrot."

"What about Santa?" Noah asked. He was a little surprised that Olive still believed in the jolly fat guy, but he sure as hell wasn't going to be the one to tell her he wasn't real.

"I asked Santa for more books." Olive gave him a sly look. "I also wrote Santa a letter for you. Daddy mailed it for me."

"Uh oh." Noah smiled. "What will I be getting this year?"

Olive shrugged. "I can't say. You'll have to wait, and I guess it depends if you've been good or not."

Noah gasped, offended. "I'm always good."

Olive narrowed her eyes. "You and Juan painted Janelle's garden gnomes to look like zombies."

"She's always planting things at my house." Noah huffed. "I was just doing her a favor."

The kitchen door opened again, and Noah recognized Grammy's nice dress shoes. She pulled the table cloth up and glared at him. "Get out from under there, Noah Benjamin Wilson."

Uh oh. She used the full name, I think. "Sorry, Grammy."

Noah and Olive climbed out from under the table, and Grammy hugged them both. "Go enjoy the party."

Noah reluctantly left the safety of the kitchen and looked around. Zed sat beside Griff and glared at Luke. The alpha that had gotten Griff pregnant was there with his girlfriend, Brittney. The man winced when he met Zed's eyes, then quickly looked away.

Noah snickered before he noticed a familiar blond and rushed off to hide again. He spent the party dodging Justin and visiting with his family and friends. He was happy to see Juan and Jackson there with Oscar.

He waved Juan over when his friend looked like he had a moment. "Will you do me a favor?" Noah asked.

"Sure," Juan said. "What do you need?"

Noah leaned forward. "Justin is trying to set me up with Griff. I like Griff, but we're just friends."

Juan eyed him. "Why not give Griff a chance?"

Noah looked away. "I'm kind of involved with someone. I think anyway."

Juan smacked his arm. "Who? Why didn't you tell me?"

"I haven't told anyone. It's too new." Noah felt his face heat. "It's not a big deal." *It was the biggest deal of his life.*

"You haven't dated anyone since, you know." Juan waved around his ears.

"Everyone is settling down," Noah said, shrugging. "I want that to but haven't met anyone until now." *Now, he couldn't imagine being with anyone but Zed.*

"I'll distract Justin," Juan said, nodding and looking around. "It may not be too hard to do."

Noah followed his gaze. Now Justin *and* Zed were glaring at Luke. "I almost feel sorry for the man."

A few hours later, Noah was beyond exhausted. He loved his family, but they could be overwhelming when everyone got together. All he wanted to do was curl into Zed's arms and close his eyes.

"Damn it, I need to tell everyone," Noah said, rubbing his eyes. "Then I could do whatever I want."

Someone patted his shoulder, and Noah jumped, then looked up. Grammy and Gramps were there, both eyeing him with curiosity.

"Tell everyone what?" Gramps asked, eyes full of mischief.

Just say it, he told himself. "I'm dating Zed."

Grammy blinked. "And?"

Noah leaned back, giving her a confused look. "We're living together, but it's just because he wants to protect me."

"And?" Grammy asked, leaning forward, eyes narrowed.

Noah frowned. "We have sex?"

Grammy nodded. "And?"

"What else do you want me to say?" Noah asked, baffled. "That's it. That's what we do."

"What about love, baby boy?" Grammy pulled him into her arms. "Are you there yet? Have you thought about adopting?"

"Grammy," he said, blushing. "It's only been a few months, and we just started dating."

Grammy arched a brow. "You've been dallying with him for months? Why are we only hearing about this now?"

"Did you say dallying?" Noah snickered. "Really?"

Gramps chuckled and looked over Noah's shoulder. "Let him go, Laurel. They'll figure it out in time."

A tap on his arm drew his attention, and he saw Zed had joined them. The other alpha's familiar, strong hands settled on his shoulders and turned him around. "We're doing this?"

Noah leaned up and kissed him, enjoying his familiar taste and warm weight of his arms around him. When he leaned back, several of his cousins were around him, laughing and speaking quickly enough he couldn't follow their lips or their signing hands.

Zed's steady presence was a comfort in the chaos, and Noah focused on him. "Are you sure, Z?"

Zed smiled his crooked smile and nodded. "Never been more certain of anything, and for the record, I'm living with you because there's no place I would rather be. Having another pair of eyes watching over the ranch is just an added bonus."

Noah felt his cheeks heat. *He wants to live with me. He really wants to be with me.*

"There must be something wrong with my eyes," Noah said, pursing his lips. "I can't take them off you."

Zed's body shook with laughter, and he kissed Noah again. "You're ridiculous."

~

LATER THAT NIGHT, NOAH FINALLY MADE HIS WAY HOME. After the Wilson party, Zed had gone to Justin's with Griff and Bea while Noah had spent Christmas evening with Elijah's family.

Zed would be home soon. *Home. It's our home now,* Noah thought.

Noah had to do some arguing to get his new patrol to take a night off, and Zed wouldn't be happy that he didn't wait for him to get to Carter's before coming home.

Noah yawned and parked his truck in front of the rescue barn before looking into the passenger seat where his present from Santa lay. The brown, white, and black pygmy goat was just a baby. Apparently, Santa had told Olive that its mother had passed away, and it needed Noah to take care of it. *Fucking jolly bastard.*

Noah got out and picked the goat up, carrying it toward the barn. He set it down while he started readying a stall for it, but the little guy had other plans.

The goat ran straight to Peanut's stall and jumped around when the miniature lowered her head to sniff him.

Noah readjusted his plans and worked on the stall next to Peanut. "I think he's another addition to the sandwich club."

After getting the little guy settled down, Noah rolled his shoulders. "Christmas shouldn't be exhausting."

He had just shut and locked the barn door when someone grabbed his shoulder and spun him around.

Noah gasped, eyes widening when the motion lights fell across Steven Wilson's face. His dad looked older, and the past three years hadn't been kind to him. In Noah's memory, his dad was large and powerful, with all the charm of Cary Grant. Now, though, he looked tired and anxious.

He's just a man, Noah reminded himself. *I can take care of myself.*

Steven scowled and pushed Noah against the door. "I should kill you… left me… useless piece of shit."

Noah slowed his breathing and tried to focus. "I can't hear, Dad. You're going to have to speak slower if you want me to speechread."

Disgust flashed across his face, and Steven pulled back his fist.

Noah moved with thinking, grabbing his dad's arm and twisting it behind his back. "I'm not a scared, confused, and injured kid anymore, Dad. Don't fuck with me, or I'll put you on the ground." The strain on his throat told him he'd likely screamed the words, but he didn't care. They were true, and it was time he remembered that.

He pushed Steven away from him, and his dad stumbled before turning back around, eyes widening in shock. He shook his head, eyes growing hard again. "I need money," he said, slower this time. "You owe me."

"I don't owe you a damn thing." Noah crossed his arms. "Get the hell out of here before I call the sheriff." Noah would hate to bother him on Christmas, but he'd promised everyone to play it safe.

Steven's shoulders slumped, and he gave Noah an

agonized look. "Do you think I want to be here? I know I hurt you and Elijah. If I could, I'd go back and change things, but I can't."

Uncertainty hit Noah. "Then why are you here?"

"Your mother left me."

Noah felt his face slacken in shock, and he put a hand on his dad's shoulder. He hadn't expected that. Rachael and Steven were two of a kind and seemed completely devoted to one another. They had their *oddities*, but everything they did was to support one another's schemes. "Why would she do that?"

Steven rubbed his eyes, face filled with sadness. "Money. Elijah and that fucking lawyer of his ruined us. I made a few deals with an old friend, but Racheal has expectations that I couldn't meet. She divorced me and remarried some old retired businessman. She won't even take my calls anymore."

Noah swallowed hard, taking a moment to process his dad's words. "I'm sorry, Dad. I wish I could help you, but I'm sure she won't talk to me anyway."

Steven gave him a soft look and patted his cheek. "You were always a sweet boy, Noah. I've got a plan to win her back, but it involves a lot of cash. I borrowed money... broke again. I was upset when she left me and... when I get upset."

Noah didn't bother to ask his dad to repeat his words. He knew exactly what he meant. When Steven Wilson got upset, he gambled. He borrowed money from shady-ass people and blew it all.

Steven's eyes watered. "I owe some bad... money... die... please, Noah."

Noah looked away for a moment, but his dad kept talking, and Noah completely lost track of the conversation. It didn't matter though. Not really. *He's in debt again.* "I don't have the kind of money you need. Everything I have goes into the horses."

Steven narrowed his eyes. "Maybe I'll go see Elijah."

Noah growled and grabbed his dad by the front of the shirt. "Don't you dare."

Steven's shoulders wilted. "I can't help it. Give me what you have, son. It will be a start, and I'll leave Hobson Hills."

Noah pulled his wallet out and handed Steven all his cash. "I'll transfer two thousand to that account you gave me. That's all I have."

It would make the next three months hard, and he would have to hold off on hiring someone new, but if it got his dad to leave them all alone, it was worth it.

Steven hugged him, then leaned back and smiled. "Good boy."

ZED YAWNED ON THE WAY HOME FROM JUSTIN'S HOUSE. Bea had been a ball of energy all day, but he had loved spending time with his brothers and the girls on Christmas.

He grinned. He had especially enjoyed explaining his relationship with Noah. *Finally.*

His lights flashed on a familiar looking car driving away from the ranch. "Oh, the fuck he didn't."

Zed pressed the gas and sped into the ranch's

driveway. He drove straight to the barns. He could see the door on the rescue barn cracked open.

He left the car running and hurried inside, looking around frantically. "Noah?" He shook his head. Noah wouldn't hear him.

The lights were dimmed, but he saw Noah's hat on top of the gate leading to the stall next to Peanut. He peeked over and let out a breath of relief.

Noah sat cross-legged in a pile of hay. A tiny pygmy goat sat in his lap, drinking from a bottle of milk.

Zed sat in front of him and waited.

Noah looked up, eyes wet. "My dad was here."

"I saw his car leaving," Zed said, face taut with anger.

"I gave him money."

Zed sighed. "Noah."

"I just wanted him to go away." Noah looked at the goat. "I was so happy today, then he came by and ruined it."

Zed scooted in closer and tilted Noah's face up. "It will be okay."

Noah pulled away. "Why do you even want me, Z? He'll come back now that he thinks I have money. You didn't ask for all of this." He waved a hand around his ear. "Maybe you should find an omega without all my baggage. That would be better for you."

Zed narrowed his eyes. "There is nothing wrong with you, Noah." He made the sign for *deaf* and then *family*. "Deaf is just one part of who you are. Your shitty parents are just one piece of your past. I want every single bit of you. I want to be your alpha, but you need to let me in."

Noah watched him, and Zed could see the struggle to trust in his eyes. "I want to believe you. I want to be your alpha too."

"Then that's what we'll be," Zed said. "Now, where the hell did the goat come from?"

CHAPTER 12

APRIL

"Okay, so that's another six kegs sent to the Irish Rose," Abel said and groaned. "Where are all these tourists coming from?" He rocked Emma in his arms as he watched Zed help load the delivery truck. "Damn, Zed, you're my favorite person. You can never leave, okay? You'll have to stay here forever."

Zed smirked. "I'm okay with that."

He had lived with Noah for months now, and he had never been happier in his life. Being with Noah felt right somehow. He felt like home to Zed.

Abel laughed. "I bet you are. You better keep treating my little cousin well too."

Zed smiled and rolled the dolly back into the brewery. "Oh, I will. Are we going to start another round of A&J?"

"I'll handle it. Go get some lunch." Abel followed behind him. "Janelle will be here in an hour, so you two can check over the farm. Emma and I will get things started while you're gone."

Zed frowned. "Are you sure? I don't mind staying."

Abel pointed to the door. "Go."

"Yes, boss." Zed laughed and grabbed his rain coat. It had started raining at the beginning of the month and had yet to stop.

He paused a moment to look over the fields nearest the brewery and felt a surge of satisfaction. For the past two months, he'd been busy nonstop with the farm and brewery, but there was something intensely satisfying about seeing his hard work coming to fruition.

The hops plants were starting to sprout up from the half-frozen ground, and he had already harvested a load of hop shoots at Janelle's direction, so she could sell them to a restaurant in Bangor. Abel and he hadn't even known a person could eat them, but the hops had needed to be thinned out anyway.

He parked in front of Griff's house and hurried to the porch through the rain. Griff met him at the door, a scowl on his face.

"Did you eat breakfast?" Zed asked, pushing past him. "How about I make you some lunch while you rest your feet?"

"I'm not helpless, Zed." Griff shoved him, then led him to the kitchen. "I'd like a grilled cheese though. No one makes them like you do."

Zed hugged his brother, then pointed at the padded rocker and ottoman in front of the window. "Prop those ankles up, and I'll get you fed. Where's Bea?"

Griff groaned as he lowered himself into the rocker. "Ray came and picked her up this morning. She's having a playdate with Min and Jun."

Zed helped him get his legs up on the ottoman. "She really likes Min, doesn't she?"

Griff smiled widely. "They adore each other. I love that she has such a good friend, and she's not even in preschool yet."

"Me too." Zed got the butter and cheese from the fridge. "I met Luke for lunch a couple of days ago."

Griff snorted. "I know. I called him afterward for a wellness check."

Zed grunted and focused on the frying pan. "He's not horrible."

"Aww, you're so sweet." Griff propped his hands on his belly. "How's Noah?" Zed couldn't help but smile, and his brother laughed at him. "You two are so cute together. I worry that you still have time to coddle me though. Do you need a pet?"

Zed gave him a flat look. "I have plenty of pets."

Griff waved a hand. "Those are all Noah's. You need a puppy or something to distract you."

"Captain Hoof lives in the house. We had to put window shelves in so my plants would be out of reach." Zed scowled when he thought of the pygmy goat. The little guy had made it clear he belonged at Noah's side *all* the time. Even the sandwich club wasn't so bad, and they followed Noah around like big puppies when he worked.

"Hmm, I'm not convinced." The corner of Griff's mouth ticked up. "Happiness looks good on you, big brother."

Zed turned the stove off, then stuffed lettuce and a

slice of tomato on the grilled cheese before bringing it to Griff. He lifted Griff's feet into his lap, sat on the ottoman, and started massaging his brother's swollen ankles.

Griff leaned back and ate his sandwich. "You're the best brother in the whole world."

"I'm telling Justin that."

"Wait," Griff said, eyes widening in panic. "He's cooking me dinner tonight, and he gives the best back rubs."

Zed chuckled. "So, I kinda did something last weekend."

Griff waggled his brows. "What did you and Noah do?"

Zed rolled his eyes. "Not that, you perv. Noah and his buddies had a Bigfoot hunting trip, so I went to the town over. You know, the one with the mall?"

Griff swallowed another bit of his sandwich. "Okay?"

Zed released the breath he hadn't realized he was holding. "I bought a ring."

Griff's mouth fell open.

Zed dug in his pocket and pulled out the small box.

Griff practically tossed his empty plate at Zed and grabbed the box. Inside were two plain gold bands.

"His is engraved." Zed fought his nervousness. "What do you think?"

Griff looked inside Noah's ring. "'Forever and always.'" He looked up, eyes watering. "Are you sure, Zed? You haven't even told him you love him."

Zed snorted. "I was waiting for him to say it first. I know he loves me, but he's damn stubborn."

Griff laughed. "You both are. When are you going to ask him?"

"Tonight." Zed put the box back in his pocket and stood. He went to the sink and washed his hands and Griff's plate. "I'm getting home a little early, so I can cook his favorite meal. Then, I'm just going to ask him."

"Tell him you love him first," Griff said, eyes narrowed. "I know it's scary, but he deserves it. Then, if he doesn't love you, I'll skin him alive. I don't even care if Gramps hides my body in the woods."

Zed grinned. "He loves me, Griff. I don't know if he'll ever admit it, but he does."

LATER THAT NIGHT, ZED TRIED TO REMIND HIMSELF THAT Noah *really* did love him. His alpha hadn't had the greatest day. Noah had dealt with bad dreams the last two nights, so he was exhausted. He was also irritable and worried.

Zed knew it would be a voice-off night so Noah could relax. He was still learning ASL, probably would always be learning it, but he could hold a conversation with Noah now.

"Stinkbug will be okay," he signed. "Doc said the surgery went well."

Noah scowled, and his hands shook with emotion as he signed. "I shouldn't have let him get hurt. I knew that fence needed patching."

Zed cut Noah a piece of apple pie and put it in front of him, before sitting back down. "You were set to fix it tomorrow, and you just found it last night."

Noah stabbed the pie with his fork and glared at Zed as he chewed.

It shouldn't make Zed want to smile, and he sure as hell wasn't amused. He hated that Noah was upset.

Captain Hoof bleated from under the table.

Noah grabbed a treat from the bowl to his right and fed it to him. "Today's been a shit day. I'm sorry I'm in a foul mood."

Zed shrugged. "They happen." He thought about the ring in his pocket. He knew now wasn't the best time. Noah needed a nice and easy night.

"Dinner was really good." Noah gave him a forced smile. "Thank you."

Zed leaned over and kissed him. "I'll do dishes. Go snuggle with Tuffy." He stood and grabbed their empty plates, then started running the dish water.

Noah's arms wrapped around him from behind, and the younger alpha stood on his tiptoes to kiss the back of Zed's neck.

Zed closed his eyes, smiling as he leaned back into Noah's arms.

Noah's hands slid under his shirt and tweaked his nipples before slowly sliding down his sides to his hips. Noah's hard dick pressed against him, and Zed's own dick stirred.

Noah froze when one of his hands glided over the box in Zed's pocket. "What's that?" he asked aloud.

"Fuck," Zed said under his breath, quickly turning around. "Nothing."

Noah's eyes narrowed. "Why are you acting so strange?" he signed.

"I'm not." Zed looked away, wincing.

Noah shook his head. "I gave you a chance to come clean," he signed. "Captain Hoof," he called out loudly. "Attack!"

"Damn it." Zed darted around Noah and ran for the stairs. He had already lost several good shirts to Noah's goat.

Captain Hoof bleated loudly and ran after him, absolutely sure that he would get more treats if he managed to get Zed on the ground.

Noah laughed hard when the goat headbutted Zed in the back of the knees, making him stumble.

Zed swore and caught the goat when he jumped toward him. Captain Hoof instantly latched onto the shoulder of his flannel shirt and started chewing. He turned around and glared at Noah.

Noah leaned against the wall, Tuffy held close to his chest as he laughed, tears pouring down his cheeks. Zed loved it. *Maybe tonight's not the wrong night.*

He carried the goat to Noah and kicked his man's shin, getting his attention.

Noah wiped his eyes on the arm of his shirt. "Good goat."

Zed set Captain Hoof down and signed the words he'd been practicing for months now. "From the first day I met you, I knew you were someone I wanted in my life. I didn't realize at the time that you would become everything to me. I love you, Noah Wilson. Will you marry me?"

He kept his eyes down as he dug the box out of his pocket and opened it. Now that he'd said all of that, he didn't want to see Noah's reaction.

He saw Tuffy settle on the floor when Noah put him down, then he felt Noah's hands cupping his face. When his eyes met Noah's, he cursed at the tears he'd caused. He hadn't wanted to upset Noah.

Noah signed, "I love you too," then leaned up and kissed him.

Zed's mouth moved over Noah's as he lost himself in his alpha's taste. He didn't even notice they were moving until he was half naked and bent over the table.

Noah licked and nibbled his way up Zed's spine until he got to his neck and bit down. Moments later, he was buried in Zed's stretched hole.

Zed gripped the edge of the table and shuddered as Noah pounded into him. Neither of them lasted long. Noah's hoarse cry signaled his release, and Zed felt him come inside him. Zed splattered his own cum on the table beneath him.

Noah panted as he leaned over and pressed his mouth to Zed's ear. "Yes."

It took far too long for Zed to figure out what he meant, but when he did, he grinned and pressed his flushed face to the table. *We're getting married.*

"Shit! Captain Hoof, don't eat that." Noah pushed up and fell back on his ass when he tripped over his pants.

Zed stood and turned around slowly, pulling up his

own pants as he did. Captain Hoof had their ring box in his mouth and darted into the living room. Zed laughed and watched Noah stumble around the kitchen, dick hanging out, as he chased their goat.

CHAPTER 13

The next morning, nothing could ruin Noah's mood. His dad texted asking for more money? Fuck him. Noah had gotten good at ignoring them. Stinkbug needed more stitches? Doc Grover was a good vet, and Noah would take care of him. The new patient hated horses? That was okay because Noah had plenty of business anyway. Tuffy brought him a half-dead rat? That was fine because Noah had Dean to deal with it while he lost his shit.

Noah shuddered when Dean walked past him with the creature. "I hate rats."

"Jules wants a pet rat. They're kind of cute."

Noah shuddered again, and Dean laughed and shook his head before heading toward one of the empty pastures. Tuffy batted at his boot before hopping onto Butter's back.

"Don't try acting cute now." He frowned at the cat before turning the water pump on and topping off the trough next to the gate. Carrot, Stinkbug, and the miniatures had their own pasture to play in. It was muddy as hell, but the horses were enjoying the rare morning sunshine.

Noah lifted his face up, soaking in the slight heat. The fresh air was a godsend after being cooped up in the house or barns for months. Of course, having Zed with him made it more bearable than usual.

He turned around and stumbled over Captain Hoof. The pygmy goat jumped around his feet, tail flitting back and forth. The little guy wore the blue and green plaid sweater that Ernie had knitted him, and his tags shook on the dark blue collar Zed had bought him. Noah flashed back to when he was a kid.

It was when they lived in an apartment in Vegas, and their neighbor had a tiny shih tzu. He had always known the dog was coming when he heard his tags jingling. He had wanted a dog so badly, but his parents were constantly on the move, so it had been impossible.

He caught Captain Hoof in his arms when he jumped high enough. *Now I have my goat.* His pocket buzzed, and he set his goat down to read the text.

Ray: We need to talk. Can I bring you lunch?

Noah winced. That sounded ominous. He texted back, then put his phone up. Ray had been watching Noah's mom and dad for a while now and kept him updated on their whereabouts. So far, all his dad had done was text him. He hadn't heard from his mother at all. Not that he was upset about it.

He took pictures of their pets and sent them to Zed and got a picture of Abel and his kids in return. After that, the morning went fast. He had a personal session with Diane after her patient left and told her about the proposal. She had danced around his office for a solid ten minutes.

Ray brought him a roast beef sandwich and some sliced pickles. They sat on Noah's tailgate next to the sandwich club's pasture.

Noah ate a bite and waited for Ray to gather his thoughts. His friend looked troubled.

Ray put his sandwich down and signed. "I keep looking into your mother's relationship with her new husband. Ted Renard is eighty-nine years old, was recently diagnosed with dementia, and is a millionaire."

Noah tilted his head and set his sandwich down so he could sign. "Alright. That's not good news, but what's the problem?"

"Right after they married, your mom got a conservatorship over him. She's legally his guardian."

Noah scowled. "That sounds like her. She married him for his money."

"Their housekeeper is worried about him," Ray signed. "Your mom dismissed his home nurse, and Renard is getting worse. There have been accidents. Suspicious accidents."

Noah shifted, uncomfortable with the realization of what was happening. "She's trying to kill him, isn't she?"

"That's what we suspect." Ray rubbed his hands over his head. "I don't know what to do with this information. I have nothing but suspicions."

"Does Renard have any other family?" Noah asked.

A look of consternation crossed Ray's face. "A son, a daughter, several grandchildren, and a few great-grandchildren. All live out-of-state."

Noah chewed on his lip. Legally, there was very little they could do unless she was caught hurting the man. If Gramps was in that position though, Noah would want to know. He'd also want to take care of the problem.

"Send everything you have to his kids," Noah signed. "Do you think they know about Mom's past?"

"As far as I can tell, they don't," Ray signed. "I'll send them everything and put the housekeeper in touch with them too."

Noah crossed his arms and nodded. "Make it so," he said aloud.

Ray laughed. "Are Olive and Elijah making you watch *Star Trek* reruns?"

"I wouldn't say they're forcing me," he signed and laughed. "Any news on Dad?"

Ray shook his head. "Nothing new. He's doing business with some bad people, but so far, they're on good terms."

Noah made a face. "Tell me good things."

Ray leaned back and grinned. "Jake told his brothers that he's asexual. They didn't even blink."

"He was worried about it."

Ray gave him a fond look. "Thank you for talking to him. Jake looks up to you."

Noah shrugged, flushing. "He's a good kid."

"So are you." Ray pulled him over and gave him a noogie, knocking Noah's hat off in the process.

"Stop it," Noah said, laughing. "Captain Hoof, attack!"

His goat looked up from where it was chewing on Ray's boot. He stared at Noah for a moment, then went back to chewing his boot.

Later that evening, Zed arrived home. Noah was just finishing the feeding and settling everyone down for the night. Zed had been getting home later than usual lately, but Noah knew it would be even worse during the summer and into the fall.

Zed yawned wide, then pulled Noah into his arms for a kiss. "Missed you," he signed once he'd let Noah go.

Noah pushed back into his arms and hugged him. "Missed you too," he said aloud. "Ray came by for lunch. He had some news about my mom." Noah quickly summed up what Ray had found out. "Do you think we did the right thing?"

Zed leaned back, expression full of worry and signed. "Yes. Maybe the man's family can do something about her. I'm sorry you're the one who had to make that decision."

Noah licked his lips. "I don't want Elijah to have to even think about them."

Zed buried his face against Noah's neck and held him for a few moments. Noah felt his stomach rumble and laughed when Zed leaned back, grinning.

"Want to go get a burger at the diner?" Noah asked.

Zed winced. "I would, but I told Justin and Griff about our engagement. They used Bea to drag it out of me. Now, they want to buy us dinner at the Irish Rose," he signed.

Noah groaned. "I better tell Elijah before he finds out. I meant to go tell him at lunch, but Ray distracted me."

His phone vibrated in his pocket, and he pulled it out to read the text.

Elijah: Well, well, well. Guess what I heard from Tanner who heard it from Justin? Get your ass ready and meet us at the Irish Rose. We have some celebrating to do.

"To Noah and Zed," Gramps said, holding his glass of beer high.

"To Noah and his hottie," Zoe called out and signed before grabbing another beer to guzzle down. Her new husband, Gib, watched her in amusement.

Noah laughed and sipped his beer. This was the tenth toast Gramps had called for, so he was getting a little tipsy. He leaned into Zed's side and looked around at all his friends and family. It was a good thing Tuesdays were the Irish Rose's slow days. Wilsons had taken over the place.

He didn't even try to keep up with the conversations going on around him. He had quickly discovered that when everyone was gathered, there was no easy way for him to follow everything. Usually one of his friends signed the highlights for him and he just relaxed and tried to enjoy the moment. It would be lonely, except his family never let him stay completely unconnected.

A grinning Marco sat in front of him and signed for Noah. "Anna wants to plan the wedding, but Griff is arguing with her because he wants to do it. Janelle is arguing with Justin about who the surrogate will be when you two decide on kids. Oh no, now Elijah's in on it. And Zoe. And Griff. Please promise me you won't let them all be your surrogates at the same time. That's a lot of kids at once. They're better spread out a bit."

Elijah stuck his tongue out at Zoe, then leaned his head on Noah's shoulder. Noah patted Elijah's belly and slid another chicken tender on his brother's plate. Elijah was at the point of his pregnancy where eating was a live action sport.

When both Elijah and Griff stood and started toward the restroom, Noah leaned close to Zed. "I'll put twenty kisses on Elijah getting to the bathroom first." The two omegas were both well into their third trimesters.

Zed narrowed his eyes and studied his brother. "Griff is bigger, but he has strong legs. I'll take that bet."

"And they're off," Marco signed quickly, face expressive as he narrated the race. "Elijah has a head start, but Griff is gaining ground fast. Oh, there's Justin to distract Griff with baby Ronnie. Always beware the babies, folks. They slow you down with those big eyes and dimples. It looks like Elijah will win. He's close, close, almost there. No! Olive moves in with a plate of

Reuben's apple bars. Apples are Elijah's one weakness, and now Griff is back in the game. He's making up for the slow start and passing Elijah right now. This race has taken a surprising turn, but the surprises aren't over. Would you look at that folks? Elijah can eat and walk at the same time. This race is getting intense. They're side-by-side and have linked arms. What kind of race is this? They're stopping to chat in front of the door. And… Griff holds the door for Elijah, letting him in for the win!"

"Yes!" Noah cheered and raised his arms in the air. "Elijah wins, so give me my kisses, Z!"

Zed's face turned an alarming shade of red as he leaned against Noah and laughed hard. He was vaguely aware of his family shooting them confused, but amused, looks but chose to ignore them.

He calmed down and paid more attention when Marco frowned, eyes looking over Noah's shoulder. His turned to Noah and Zed, hands moving quickly. "The sheriff just came in and looked around until he saw Zed. He looks upset."

Noah sat up, turning around to watch the door. Zed did the same and they watched the sheriff weave his way through the crowded pub.

Sheriff McKenzie pulled a chair up to their table and sat. He didn't know ASL, but he had worked hard to pick up enough Signed English to communicate with Noah. "There is a problem."

"My dad?" Noah asked aloud. By the looks he garnered, he had been a little too loud. Everyone at their table watched them now.

"No," Sheriff McKenzie signed. "Zed. Brothers. Sister."

Noah shared a confused look with Zed. "What?" Noah asked. "It's okay if you need to speak, Sheriff. Zed can explain it to me if I can't speechread."

McKenzie took his hat off and rubbed a hand over his salt and pepper hair. He was a little older than Noah's Uncle Barry, but he wore his age well.

"An hour ago, I pulled a car over. Tags were out of date." He paused and gave Noah a questioning look.

"I'm good." Noah nodded. "You can go on."

McKenzie spoke a little too fast. "Driver was underage. Fifteen and only had a… two other kids… a toddler… and a… in the front."

Noah didn't catch everything the sheriff said, but he got enough to know there were three kids in the car and an underage driver.

"The oldest—" McKenzie paused to spell out the name for Noah. *Seth*. "Seth said they were on the way to live with their brother."

"Why were they driving?" Zed signed first, then asked the sheriff aloud.

McKenzie looked uncomfortable. "He wouldn't say. I'll contact social services if needed. They're outside now."

"Why bring them here?" Noah asked. "Who is their brother?"

McKenzie nodded at Zed. "They told me his name was Zed Ames and he worked at Abel's Farm and Brewery. They had a… and picture."

"A what?" Noah asked, eyes wide. Zed had more

brothers. Why the hell would Joshua Ames keep having kids if he couldn't even raise his first three? *Fuck, Justin, Griff, and him are going to take this hard.*

"The article in the local brewery magazine has a picture of me," Zed signed, face white. The corners of his mouth were pulled down, and his eyes looked strained.

Noah set his beer on the table and took Zed's hand. "Okay. There are three kids outside waiting to meet their brother. What do you want to do?"

Zed's eyes hardened as he signed. "I want to kill Joshua Ames. What should we do?"

Noah leaned forward and kissed him. "You'll be the awesome big brother that you always are. Go on outside. I'll hunt down Griff and Justin and meet you there."

CHAPTER 14

Zed's hands shook as he followed the sheriff outside. He stuffed them in his coat pockets and swallowed hard. *What the fuck did you do now, Dad?*

Sheriff McKenzie glanced at him over his shoulder. "I'll be honest with you here, Ames. I ran the plates when I pulled them over. They're from Delamont, Indiana, and were reported missing by the police. I called and left a message with the department, but no one has gotten back with me yet. I know your dad's history, and these three kids look like they've been on their own for at least a few days. I'll have to talk to social services in the morning to sort everything out, but I'll give you tonight to figure out what the fuck is going on."

"Thanks," Zed said, voice hoarse. "I'll get it sorted."

"You have help if you need it." McKenzie nodded back toward the pub. "Those people in there care. Hell, you're lucky they're giving you space right now. Don't expect it to last."

Zed smiled softly, thinking about the certainty in Noah's eyes when he'd held Zed's hand. His alpha would stand with him, no matter what. He knew that as well as he knew his brothers would help him too.

A nervous teenager leaned against McKenzie's car, arms crossed as he shivered in the thin, long-sleeved shirt he wore. The omega looked a lot like Zed had when he was a kid. He even had the big ears. *Seth.*

Beside him was a young girl of about eight. Her long blond hair hung in two braids, and her brother's coat hung over her hands. She had a baby in her arms. A little boy by the looks of things.

McKenzie waved his hand toward them. "This is Seth, Mary, and Pike." He took off his coat and handed it to Seth. "You could have waited in the car, kid. It would have been warmer."

"You're Zed. Our brother," Seth said, shrugging into the coat. His narrow shoulders slumped in relief either at Zed's presence or the warmth of the heavy jacket. "Mom told me to come to you if something happened."

"What happened?" Zed said, keeping his voice soft.

"Mom..." Seth's voice broke and his eyes watered. "Mom did something bad. Before she did, she stuck us in the car and told me to get to you."

Zed heard gravel crunch behind him and breathed a little easier when Noah's hand slipped into his. He looked toward his alpha, glad the evening sun hadn't set yet. "This is Seth, Mary, and Pike." He fingerspelled the names for him. "My brothers and sister."

Noah smiled. "I'm Noah, Zed's fiancé. This is Justin and Griff, your other brothers."

"Can you tell us what your mom did?" Zed asked, then signed for Noah's benefit.

Seth looked at the sheriff, body shaking. "Can Mary and Pike go inside? They don't know."

"I wanna know what happened," Mary said, voice sullen. "I'm not a baby."

"Mary, Pike may be cold and hungry," Justin said softly. "I can get you two something to eat while Seth explains things. I have a little girl about Pike's age and Griff's daughter, Bea, has some new coloring books. Do you want to meet them?"

"Yes, please. Can I?" Mary looked to Seth and waited until he nodded before going with Justin.

Justin gave Zed a hard look. "You *will* tell me what's going on later. You and Griff can't keep this from me too."

Zed frowned. *What the hell is he talking about?* "Of course."

A flash of hurt crossed Justin's face before he leaned closer. "You and Griff always tell me things last."

Understanding hit him like a punch in the gut. He hadn't told Justin about his feelings for Noah until the last minute, and Griff had told Justin about the baby weeks after he had told Zed. Sometimes, Zed forgot it wasn't just him and Griff against the world anymore.

"I'm sorry, Justin. I promise I'll tell you everything tonight."

Justin nodded and steered Mary inside. "I think I'll like having a sister, Mary. Do you like rabbits or guinea pigs? I have one of each."

Zed watched them leave and had to fight a smile.

His dad was a piece of shit, but the man had given him Griff and Justin. He looked at Seth. *He apparently gave us three more too.*

"Okay," Griff said slowly once the others were gone. "Can you tell us what happened?"

Seth licked his lips and shuffled his feet. "Dad told us about his kids – Zed, Justin, and Griffin. He told us you all hated him because your moms turned you against him, but he tried to keep up with you all. He bought that magazine when he heard Zed and his boss were interviewed in it."

Zed's gut churned, and he squeezed Noah's hand. He didn't know how he felt about that.

"He screwed around a lot on Mom," Seth said suddenly, voice rising. "He would yell at her afterward, like it was her fault somehow. Last Thursday, we got home from school and our stuff was packed up in the car. Pike was already in his car seat. Mom told me that I needed to take them and go to Maine. She gave me the address of the brewery and her phone so I could use the GPS. She also gave me two hundred dollars. I don't know where she got it from. Dad was always complaining about being broke."

"So you came here." Griff gave him a nervous smile. "Do you have your license?"

Seth glanced at McKenzie again. "No, but I have my learner's permit. She just told us to go and went back inside. I got Mary strapped in, but I wanted to check on Mom. She was acting strange. I went to the front door. It was open, and I saw her. Dad was yelling at her, and she had a gun."

Seth started shaking again, and Zed couldn't stop himself. He pulled Noah with him and went to his brother, pulling the kid between him and Noah, so they could both hug him.

"It'll be okay," Noah said a little too loudly. Zed thought he probably had lost track of the conversation, but Noah would know Seth was upset.

Seth buried his head against Noah's chest and hugged Zed's arm. "Mom shot him. She shot him a lot, and he didn't move."

"Shit," Griff said and wiggled into the hug. "I'm so sorry, Seth."

"He was your dad too," Seth said, voice thick with tears. He hugged Zed's arm harder. "I hated him, but he was ours."

Zed was vaguely aware of McKenzie's phone ringing. The sheriff stepped away to take the call.

"She didn't even look up when I yelled," Seth whispered. "She just… She just put it to her head."

Noah stroked a hand over Seth's head and watched Zed, eyes sad. "You're going to be okay," he said again. "Zed's here now."

Zed nodded, swallowing the lump in his throat. "I'll take care of everything, and we'll get you three home."

"We can't go back there." Seth shook his head and hid his face against Noah. "We can't."

"You won't." Griff's voice was hard. "You'll go home with Zed, Justin, or me. You're our family, and we don't leave our family."

Sheriff McKenzie came closer. "That was the

Delamont police. They're happy to know you three are safe and will give you a call in the morning."

"They're dead?" Seth asked, face still buried.

"Yes." McKenzie winced. "I'm sorry, Seth."

"I don't want to think about it." Seth hugged them tighter. "I don't want to think at all."

Noah startled and looked down. "Your stomach growled. You need food."

"I'm not hungry." Seth didn't look up.

"Noah is deaf, Seth. You have to look at him for him to see what you say." Zed stroked his brother's back. "Are you sure you can't eat? They make a good burger here."

Seth looked up at Noah. "Do you sign? My friend Riley uses ASL."

Noah nodded. "Do you sign?"

"A little," Seth said, voice small. "I guess I should eat."

Zed, Griff, and Noah kept ahold of Seth, but somehow, the group moved toward the pub.

"I should warn you, Seth." Noah patted Seth's back. "My whole family is in there, and they may hug you."

Griff snorted. "They *will* hug you."

"Why is your whole family here?" Seth asked, making sure to look at Noah as he spoke.

"Engagement party." Noah leaned over and kissed Zed.

Seth gave Zed a worried look. "We can stay with you? Noah, you won't mind?"

Noah shook his head. "I don't mind. Zed accepts me and all my family. I can certainly accept all of his."

Zed smiled. Noah didn't even ask Zed if he *wanted* the kids there. He knew him well enough to know it wasn't a matter of want. Zed would do what he needed to do to take care of his family.

~

HE WATCHED NOAH TUCK MARY AND TUFFY INTO THE bed Olive usually took when she stayed over. Zed's alpha turned the night light on and made sure Mary's stuffed octopus was tucked under the covers too before kissing her forehead and tiptoeing toward Pike's crib. Elijah had donated a crib, and it was currently tucked next to the door.

Zed leaned over Pike and smoothed a hand over the baby's round belly. He was about six months old and a complete cutie with dark brown curls and warm brown eyes.

Noah and he left the door cracked before they went to Seth's room next door. The teen was sleeping hard, exhaustion from the emotional drain knocking him out. Captain Hoof lay at the bottom of the bad. The small goat's dark eyes watched them curiously, but he didn't bother moving.

Noah had called in Diane to talk a little with Seth, and Zed fully planned on making sure his brother had people to talk to. No one should have seen the things Seth had.

Zed left Seth's door cracked too and pulled Noah down the hall to their own room. They hadn't had a moment of privacy since early that morning.

"Okay," he signed. "Tell me what you think."

Noah gave him a sad look and signed. "I'm sorry about your dad, Z."

Zed looked away for a moment. He still didn't know how to feel about his dad. He may not know for a while. All he felt was tired and sad.

Noah's arms wrapped around him, and he sank against him. They stayed like that for a while, and Zed let himself rest. *Griff and Justin still think I take care of Noah.* He shook his head. Noah was his rock as much as he was Noah's.

He leaned back and took a breath before signing. "I want to keep the kids."

"Me too," Noah signed. "They need someone, and Griff and Justin both have kids. We'll love them and make sure they're safe and healthy."

"Are you sure?" Zed winced as he signed. "I know this wasn't the plan. Life might be easier for you if –"

Noah shook his head and pulled Zed's hands down. "Now I know how you felt when we started dating," he said aloud. "Don't be stupid. We're together in this. All the way. That's what loving someone is about." He let go of Zed's hands. "I'll talk to Uncle Marco and Uncle Bennett tomorrow. They're still foster parents and have adopted three kids now. They're actually legally adopting Tomás now too, even if he is an adult, so make that four. Maybe they can help us."

Zed chuckled. "Marco offered to take them in temporarily if they had to go to a foster home until we figured things out. I love your family," he signed.

"They love you too." Noah traced his mouth. "I love

you. I wish I would have told you sooner. I think I've loved you since I met you."

"Damn it, Noah. The things you do to me." Zed kissed him softly and pushed him down onto the bed, covering his body with his own.

"Are you my phone charger?" Noah asked, nipping at Zed's chin. "Because without you, I'd die."

Zed snorted out a laugh, then covered Noah's mouth with his own.

Noah rolled his shoulders, then grabbed the last two bags of feed from the truck and held them over his shoulder. Mary tugged her tiny work gloves up her wrists, then picked up the last small bag of goat treats and put it over her shoulder. Together, they carried their load to the feed room at back of the rescue barn.

Mary had been his constant companion since the kids arrived two days ago. She seemed content with the quiet but had happily started learning some signs from Noah and Olive.

Noah worried about her. Seth was pretty open with his feelings about losing his parents, but Mary hadn't said anything when they'd told her. She'd just hugged Noah and asked to play with Tuffy.

The funeral for their parents was next week, and neither one of them wanted to go. Zed and Noah were both conflicted on whether they should ask them to or not.

Noah tossed the bags of feed onto the growing pile and chuckled when Mary tossed her bag onto her own little stack of treats and other lighter weight supplies. "Supply day is hard work, Mary. Do you need a break?"

She chewed on her lip and nodded. "Can we play with Peanut?"

Noah scooped her up and hugged her before spinning her around. "That sounds fun."

They could really use some fun too. Yesterday, it had taken hours to finish with the people in Delamont. The police wanted to know what Seth saw, but there wasn't a question of what had happened. The evidence was clear. They'd follow up with them, but that was the easy part.

The hard part had been the lawyers and child services. It had taken Sheriff McKenzie, Diane's letter of recommendation, and several of Uncle Bennett and Uncle Marco's contacts within child services to ensure that the kids would stay with Zed for the time being. He really hadn't wanted them to have to go a foster home while the courts figured their shit out.

Denise, the kids' mom, had planned ahead enough to make a will, but the fact she murdered her husband complicated things.

For now, though, the kids were with Zed and Noah, and he had every intention of making sure it stayed that way.

Noah grabbed the brushes and a bag of hair bows before opening Peanut's stall. Mary had taken a liking to the pintaloosa, and, of course, Peanut loved being loved.

He handed Mary a brush, and she started running it through Peanut's mane. She watched Noah as he brushed down Peanut's rump and side.

She patted Peanut's back to get his attention, and he looked up, smiling. "Mommy and Daddy are dead."

Noah's smile faded, and he nodded. "Yes, sweetheart. I'm sorry."

"Is it…" She seemed to struggle with the words but kept her face tilted up toward Noah instead of looking away. "Is it my fault?"

Noah set the brush down and skirted around Peanut so he could kneel in front of May. "No, Mary. You didn't do anything wrong." *Fuck, what do I say? How do I explain this?*

She looked down, mumbling something, so he tilted her chin up. "Remember, sweetheart. I need to see your face to speechread."

"Sorry," she said, then signed *I'm sorry*.

He hugged her, then leaned back. "It's okay. Now, why would you think it was your fault?"

"Mommy was upset," Mary said, then waited for Noah to nod before continuing. "I wouldn't clean my room, and Daddy kept yelling at me."

Noah wanted to growl at the thought of anyone yelling at her, but he could admit to himself, he was a little attached to Mary. He may not have the clearest head here.

"Mommy got mad at me too." Mary's lip trembled, and she spoke a little too fast for him to read the rest of her words.

"Can you repeat that last part for me, Mary? I'm sorry."

Mary patted his cheek. "It's okay. Mommy told me I was selfish and lazy. She said I made her sad all the time."

Now Noah wanted to yell at Denise. "I think maybe your mom was upset about something else when she said those things."

"But she said them," Mary said, eyes watering. "Then she died."

He closed his eyes and hugged her as her small body shook with her sobs. Peanut nuzzled her arm and leaned against them, offering what comfort she could.

"I'm sorry they died, Mary, but I'm so happy you're here," he said against her ear. He really hoped he was whispering like he thought he was. "I don't think you're selfish or lazy. I know your mom loved you too. She sent you to Zed, and he's the absolute best person in the whole world."

Mary leaned back, face red and eyes swollen from crying. "You won't leave. Right? You and Zed won't die, will you?"

Shit, shit, shit, he thought. *What do I say to that?* He licked his lips. "We'll be here for a good long while, M."

She wiped her eyes. "I like it here. Peanut and Tuffy are my friends, and Olive is nice too."

Noah hugged her again, then stood. "Let's finish pampering Peanut. You know Jelly and Butter want their turns too."

Mary smiled shyly and nodded. "Okay."

A few hours later, he left Mary with Olive in the

living room. The two were playing some game on the Xbox. Mary would start school next week, even though there was only a month left in the semester. Noah was glad Olive would be there to make sure she settled in.

Connor, Bea, Min, Cooper, and Captain Hoof chased each other around the house, stumbling over toys as they went. Olive and the twins had donated a couple of boxes of toys and books for Mary and Pike. Connor had even spent half an hour trying to show the baby how to play with his ABC Carrybag. None of them had the heart to tell him Pike was too young for the toy.

Noah's house had never been so cluttered, and he kind of couldn't wait for Zed to get home and see it. He wanted to see his alpha's eye twitch.

Elijah puttered around the kitchen making lunch while Noah changed Pike's diaper on the fold-up card table he used for poker nights.

Noah's eyes watered. "Are they supposed to smell this bad?"

Elijah's body shook as he laughed and nodded. "Welcome to fatherhood."

Pike smiled around the fist in his mouth, and Noah couldn't help but smile back. "You stink like a decomposing, beached whale, Pike, but I still love you."

Elijah tapped the table to get his attention. Noah looked up.

"Where's Seth?" Elijah asked.

"He went to work with Zed today. I think Z wanted them to have bonding time."

"Are you really okay with all of this?" Elijah signed, shooting guilty looks toward Mary and Pike.

Noah took his time and really thought about it. He'd do what he had to because Zed's family was Noah's family, but he found that he truly enjoyed the kids being here.

"I like spending time with Olive and the twins," he finally signed. "This is different, but it's just as good. It's new though. Ask me again in a month, and we'll see if that changes." He really didn't think it would, but the kids had only been there two days.

Elijah kissed his cheek. "I love you," he said aloud.

Noah finished fastening Pike's diaper, then gave his brother a hug and gently rubbed his large baby bump. "Love you too. You'll show me how to be a good dad, right?"

Elijah's eyes lit up. "I'm the big brother, aren't I? It's my job."

LATER THAT NIGHT, NOAH LEFT THE KIDS IN THE HOUSE with Marco and Bennett and worked on finishing up his chores.

Dean had stepped up to work with Diane and the three patients scheduled for the day. Noah had never been so glad he'd hired the man, even part-time. He'd make him full-time in a heartbeat, but Dean worked full-time for Marco, and there was only one Dean to go around, damn it.

I need more help. With more patients, he finally felt like he could hire another employee.

The lights flickered on and off, and he looked up, smiling when he saw Emmet at the door.

"Where's your little partner?" Emmet asked once he'd moved closer. Noah had sent him pictures of Mary in her overalls and straw hat earlier that day.

Noah nodded hello. "She wanted to play with Tuffy. Uncle Marco and Uncle Bennett are watching Mary and Pike now. You and Saul need to come meet everyone. You'll love them."

"Do you need help with furniture or painting?" Emmet asked.

Noah shook his head. "Pike's room is all that's left to finish up. Yesterday, everyone came and got Seth and Mary's rooms ready. I never realized kids needed so much furniture."

Sadness flashed in Emmet's eyes before he managed to hide it. "That's what I hear. Do you need any help around here? Saul and I have more free time than we know what to do with."

They already did so much, so Noah almost told him no, but something stopped him. He thought of Zed and how much he liked staying busy. Emmet worked at his dad's hardware store a few towns over, and Saul worked as a mechanic about two hours away. They seemed to enjoy the ranch a lot and spent more days here than not.

"Would you or Saul be interested in a job here?" he asked aloud.

Emmet blinked in surprise. "I know I would. My

dad is retiring and my brother's taking over the store. We don't get along. I think Saul wants to make a move too."

It took him a minute to process Emmet's words, but Noah liked the idea of having Saul and Emmet closer to him. "Come to dinner tonight and bring Saul. We'll talk about it."

Emmet smiled widely. "You just want us to change diapers, don't you?"

"It crossed my mind." Noah made a face. "Babies are cute, but they stink. If you don't mind helping, I'm a little behind in bringing the horses in. I don't like leaving them out overnight. It still gets a little too cold."

"I'm on it." Emmet spun around and headed for the doorway where Zed stood watching them, Pike on his hip. The two men fist bumped, then Zed slowly walked toward Noah.

Why does he look like he's stalking me? Noah emptied the bin of food into Roger's feed bowl and eyed Zed warily. *Carrying a baby shouldn't be sexy.*

Zed smirked and slid into Noah's space, wrapping an arm around him and bringing him in for a kiss, then leaning back so Noah could speechread. "How many kids do Marco and Bennett have in total?"

"A million," Noah answered quickly. "Are they all here?"

"Yeah." Zed kissed him again. "Tomás and Shawn are painting Pike's new room, and the rest are hanging out with Seth and Mary."

Noah nodded. "Elijah and his brood were here this afternoon. I don't think we're going to have any privacy for a while. I'm sorry my family is a little overwhelming."

Zed gave him a soft look. "I'm not complaining. It's not like Griff and Bea aren't here too. Even Justin, Ronnie, and Tanner showed up. Why do you think Pike and I came to the barn?"

"Can we just stay here?" Noah asked and tickled Pike's sides. The baby's face lit up with laughter.

He was too busy laughing at Pike to see what Zed said. When the other alpha stiffened and spun around, Noah turned around. The barn door was open, and Marco had Noah's dad pinned to it, hand wrapped around his throat.

Shit, Noah thought and followed Zed to the two men.

Noah couldn't tell what Marco was saying, but Steven's face was white and full of fear. When he saw Noah, a dark little wiggle of cruelty flashed in his eyes. "Son," he said. "Help me."

Steven tried to say something else, but his lips moved too fast. It didn't matter though. He was there for one reason – money. Steven didn't care that Noah had three children now or that he was getting married. He wasn't cooking dinner for Noah and Zed so that they could catch their breath. He hadn't hauled over furniture for the kids. He wasn't painting Pike's room. He hadn't texted Noah a thousand times today to ask if he needed anything.

He didn't care a single bit about Noah or Elijah. For once, it was very clear to Noah that Steven Wilson wasn't his family. He wasn't Noah's dad.

"Shut up," Noah said aloud and pulled his phone out. "Why can't you just go away and stay gone? You ruin everything. Elijah and I aren't afraid of you, and we don't care about you anymore. You lost us. Now, I'm texting Sheriff McKenzie, and if you're still here when he arrives, I don't give a fuck if you rot in jail."

Steven snarled and started to say something, but Noah didn't care. He turned around and sent a quick text to McKenzie. By the time he turned back around, Steven was gone, and Marco and Zed watched him with wide eyes.

Noah sighed and hugged Marco, trying to push away the guilt shooting up in his gut at the words he had spoken. He wasn't responsible for Steven Wilson. "You're my dad. You've been there for me since I moved here. I'm done with him. Completely and utterly done."

Marco's arms tightened around him, and Noah let himself enjoy the dad hug. Marco was so good at them. He jumped a little when Zed hugged him from behind but settled easily, until Pike gave him a slobbery kiss on the cheek.

"Eww, baby drool." Noah made a face and wiped his cheek before grabbing Pike to press kisses all over his chubby face.

Marco's laugh shook his body. "Get used to it," he signed. "Babies drool a lot."

A COUPLE OF DAYS LATER, NOAH LOUNGED ON THE

couch and watched a movie with Zed's arm stretched over his shoulders. Mary leaned against Noah as she sat beside him with Tuffy, and Pike slept in his lap. Seth and Captain Hoof shared the recliner.

The lights were dimmed, the room smelled like slightly burned popcorn, and toys were still strewn all around the room. Noah loved it. It was a soft and quiet moment after a hectic week.

He turned and watched Zed. His alpha was focused on the show, brow furrowed in concentration. Noah felt a surge of affection for him. He loved the man, but he respected the hell out of him too. Zed was a calm and steady presence and a natural nurturer.

Despite being thoroughly loved and spoiled by the Wilson family for the past three years, Noah was well aware other families weren't always as accepting and loving. His parents had sold him out in a heartbeat for a small monthly check, and most people wouldn't have taken in three surprise siblings.

People like Zed, Elijah, and Marco were meant to be cherished. Noah would do his damnedest to make sure Zed knew how valuable he really was. For now, he would relish this happy moment.

A horrible stench wafted from Pike. *Damn it!*

Noah wrinkled his nose and stood. Zed started to get up too, but Noah waved him away. Mary just wiggled closer to Zed and settled her head against her brother.

Noah wished he could take a picture of the two, but his eyes were watering and he was sure the paint would start peeling from the walls soon.

He held Pike away from him and carefully walked up the stairs, only stumbling once. By the time he made it to the changing table in the hallway, he was gagging. "Pike, what did we feed you today?"

Drool dribbled down Pike's chin as he grinned. Noah's eyes widened, and he whimpered when he saw a trail of watery brown shit slowly running down the baby's plump leg.

"Zed," he screamed, throat aching at the volume.

Seconds later, Zed tripped up the stairs, Seth, Mary, and Captain Hoof hard on his heels. Zed gave him a panicked, scared look. "What's wrong?"

Noah shuddered and handed him Pike. "I'm going to puke."

CHAPTER 16

Zed scowled as he tugged on the strap of one of the bags he carried. "Why the hell am I here?"

Carter gave him a dry look. "I ask myself that same question every time they drag me out here."

Noah grinned and leaned up to kiss him before following Juan and a very pregnant Ernie with his own bags of equipment. *Oh yeah. That's why I'm here. A break from the kids is supposed to be nice, right?*

Carter, Mateo, and Zed brought up the rear of the group. The sun was getting low in the sky, and they'd been tromping through the woods for a good three hours.

"Does Ernie really need to be out here?" he whispered to Carter and Mateo.

"Not at all. In fact, Reuben will likely be waiting on us when we get back. He's going to be pissed." Mateo seemed unconcerned. "Don't worry too much though. Juan is taking it real slow, and if you watch, him and

Noah are hovering over Ernie instead of focusing on the woods. They won't find Bigfoot that way, but Ernie was desperate to get out of the house."

Zed noticed Noah's hands stretched out behind Ernie, like he'd catch him if he were to fall back. Juan spent more time shuffling his feet and watching Ernie than the tree line. "Okay, I see what you mean. Wait." He slowly turned his head to look at Mateo. "You actually think they'll find Bigfoot one day?"

Mateo gave him a puzzled look. "Of course. We have the right equipment, we've found signs of him before, and it's the right time of the year for it. He'll be foraging a lot right now."

Zed shared an amused look with Carter. "Okay. Good points."

"Oh my god, guys!" Ernie danced in place. "Look! It's a Bigfoot nest."

Juan grinned. "Mateo, let's take some samples." He paused a moment to sign for Noah. "Noah, you and Carter set up a perimeter. We don't want to be surprised." Juan looked at Zed. "Newbie, get the scouting cameras out and set them up around the nest. We'll leave them overnight and see what we have."

Zed sighed and lowered his packs to the ground. "I guess this is better than changing Pike's diapers or listening to Seth lament his broken heart." Seth had dated a boy for a whole week before he got dumped. Now, Zed's brother was convinced he would never love again.

He put the motion activated cameras in place and did his best to hide them in case Bigfoot was anti-technology. The *nest* Ernie had found was a hollowed-out portion of the ground under a big red maple tree. It looked like a bear den.

"Let's get out of here before Bigfoot gets back," Juan said, looking around warily. "We don't want to scare him." After he finished speaking, he signed his words to Noah and clapped Zed's alpha on the back. "I think we'll find him this time." Juan's eyes narrowed on Zed as he kept his arm wrapped around Noah. "Newbie, you and I need to talk."

Carter snickered and helped Noah watch over Ernie as they headed back to the cabin.

Mateo gave him a sympathetic look, then left him behind with Juan.

Juan eyed him. "I haven't been as attentive as I should have been the last few months as Jackson and I have been settling in together. Then there's Oscar and my papa distracting me from my duties as one of Noah's best friends."

Zed smiled. "Considering we're getting married next month, live together, share pets, and have pretty much adopted three kids, I think it's a little late to ask about my intentions."

Juan rolled his eyes. "Believe me, if you didn't have the right intentions, Gramps and Marco would have taken care of you by now. No, this is about caring for Noah. Ray, Carter, Ernie, and I have been with him for over three years now. I carried him out of that fucking joke of a hospital and watched him struggle to adapt to his loss of hearing. I got to see him thrive with that horse ranch of his. We all did. Well, not

Mateo and Niccolo. They're new to our group, but so are you."

"I owe you for what you did for him," Zed said quietly. There was no way in hell he could ever not like Elijah and the others that had rescued Noah. *I owe them everything.*

Juan shrugged. "You don't owe any of us for that. We did it for him, not you." He pulled a small notebook out of his pack. "Anyway, we got together and made this for you."

Zed stopped walking and looked at the cover in the late afternoon light. *The Care and Feeding of Noah Wilson.* "What is this?"

"Things we've learned about Noah." Juan pushed him forward to get him walking again. "His favorite recipes and foods are in there. All of his hobbies and quirks. That we've noticed anyway. Did you know he likes concerts?"

Zed frowned. "Concerts?"

"He likes heavy metal." Juan tapped the notebook. "See, you have a lot to learn to properly care for our Noah."

Zed smiled slowly. "It's my favorite subject."

He talked with Juan all the way back to Ernie and Reuben's cabin. By the time they got there, the sun had almost set.

Ernie's husband, Reuben, glowered from the porch. The man was a little bigger than Zed and had a great smile, which he wasn't sharing at the moment. *Shit, I should have made Ernie stay home.*

Zed cleared his throat and stood straighter.

Juan snickered. "Noah was right. You really do have a bro crush on Rueben."

"He's a genius," Zed hissed and shoved Juan. "Shut up."

Noah looked over his shoulder with a knowing smirk, and Zed scowled, hating that his cheeks were heating up.

"Do you want his autograph?" Carter asked, voice teasing.

Zed smiled softly when Juan stood in the porch light and signed for Noah. He had noticed Noah's friends always assigned a person to keep Noah caught up on their conversations when there were more than four of them.

"Who's autograph?" Reuben asked, frowning.

Zed's eyes widened. "Ernie wants your autograph."

Ernie leaned against Noah and giggled. "Yeah, sure I do."

"I got your back, man." Mateo wrapped an arm around Zed's shoulders. "Reuben, will you show Zed here how to make Cornish pasties? Ernie said he was hungry."

Ernie giggled harder, but Zed's heartbeat picked up. *Please, sweet baby Jesus, let me cook with Reuben.*

Reuben shrugged. "Sure. I have some groceries here. You all hungry?"

"THEN, HE SAID THAT YOU HAVE TO SEPARATE THE butter with your fingers when you make a puff pastry,"

Zed said, trying not to talk too fast. "He said that makes a big difference. I don't know why, but if he said it, then it's true."

Noah snickered and kissed the top of Mary's head. Zed's little sister held Tuffy in her arms. The cat was dressed in a bib and baby bonnet and seemed one hundred percent okay with it.

"We brought you all leftovers. Seth, I know you're hungry. I'll go ahead and warm a couple up."

Seth smiled sheepishly and signed, "Thank you." The teen was *always* hungry.

Zed bounced Pike in his arms, smiling when the baby giggled.

The strobe lights from the door flickered when the doorbell rang, and Zed waved Noah away and went to see who it was.

He frowned when he opened the door to find Ray. "Why did you ring the bell? You usually come in the back."

Ray gave him a strained smile. "I have some news for Noah. I hate this, man. I know he's going to get upset, and I just fucking hate it."

Zed sighed and held the door open. "His dad or his mom?"

"Both." Ray grabbed Pike as he walked past him. "I need some baby cuddles. I should have brought Jun with me."

Zed shut the door behind him and flipped the locks. He hated that Steven Wilson still had power over Noah, even if Noah claimed differently. The man was a piece of work, and it had been satisfying as hell to hear Marco threaten him that last day.

Noah had never asked what Marco had said, so Zed hadn't volunteered the information. Noah probably didn't need to know all the graphic threats his uncle had made.

Seth was already digging into a plate of pasties when they made it to the kitchen. Captain Hoof stood watching him, eyes hungry. Zed knew some of those pasties would make it to the goat.

Noah's smile faded when Ray signed, "We need to talk."

"Back porch," Noah said. "Seth, will you watch Mary and Pike?"

He looked between them, suspicious, then signed, "Do you need my help, Noah?"

Noah smiled and hugged the young omega. "We'll be okay. Eat your pasties."

Mary gently set Tuffy on the floor and held her arms up. "I'll hold Pike."

The cat glared at the baby as Zed passed him to Mary.

Zed followed the two men to the back porch. He had covered it in potted plants and windchimes. Noah didn't seem to mind, though he had tripped over a plant a couple of times. He had only cursed for a few minutes, though, so Zed knew he loved them.

The sound of rushing water surrounded them. The creek was a little flooded from all the spring rain, and the sound of water mixed with the tinkling of the windchimes. Zed sighed happily. He loved their home.

Ray made sure he stood facing the porch light so Noah could see him sign. "I have two pieces of information about your mom and dad."

Noah shook his head. "They're not my mom and dad," he said aloud. "They're just two people I had to spend time with."

Ray nodded, understanding in his eyes. "Alright," he signed. "First, Rachael was arrested for attempted murder. Renard's kids were *very* interested in the information I sent them. They hired someone to watch her, and they caught her in the act of trying to push him down the stairs."

"Fuck," Zed said, disbelief filling him. Based on her treatment of Elijah and Noah, he had known she was shit, but murder was something else.

Noah nodded, face empty of emotion. "I'm glad they caught her. Is Renard okay?"

"He'll be alright," Ray signed. "His kids are keeping a closer eye on him."

"Good." Noah leaned against Zed, and he took the hint and wrapped his arms around his alpha. "What about Steven?"

Ray made a face before he started signing. "My boss knows what I do on the side, so he knew I was keeping tabs on Steven. A contact of his wants to pull Steven in to testify against the assholes he's dealing with. They're promising him immunity for any crimes he's committed involving them."

Noah's mouth dropped open. "That's… Ray, that's amazing. He could get away from that shit and try to kick his gambling problem."

"He won't take their calls," Ray signed. "We thought you may have more luck with him, but only if you want to try. No pressure here."

Noah pulled his phone out and hurriedly typed out a message and hit send. "He'd be an idiot to say no to that deal. I know the kind of people he usually deals with and there's only two ways you end it with them."

"Death or prison," Ray signed. "Otherwise, they have their hooks in you for life."

"He has a chance though." Noah's phone buzzed and his face lit up. "It's him." The hope slowly drained from his face. "He says he has things under control, and there's no need to worry. Then he asked for a couple grand." He looked up, bitterness twisting his mouth. "Of course, he doesn't want out. I don't know why I thought he might."

Ray blew out a breath, then hugged Noah. "I love you, little alpha. I wish this was easier for you."

Noah smiled dryly. "They've been doing horrible things my whole life. I'm done with it all now. Dad… no, Steven, had the chance to change, but he didn't. Fuck him." He took Zed's hand and gave him a long look. "I have a family, and they're my priority. It's time I look to the future and not the past."

Something warm settled in Zed. He liked being Noah's priority.

Noah rolled his neck and shoulders and took a big breath. "Now, I have to go meet Carter for one last chore for the night. Seth's coming with, so you'll have to get Pike and Mary to bed by yourself, Z."

Zed frowned. "What's going on?"

Noah's smile was full of mischief. "We're dressing Ernie's alpacas up like Bigfoot. It's payback for putting Stinkbug in a poodle costume and sending pictures to everyone."

Zed nodded, eyes hard. "I'll protect the home front. Avenge Stinkbug's honor, my love."

CHAPTER 17

JUNE

Zed looked at himself in the mirror. "I really look alright?" He wore a navy-blue suit with a boutonniere of daisies on his lapel. His beard was trimmed and his hair slicked back.

"You're so handsome." Griff sniffled and wiped his eyes. "I can't believe you're getting married."

Justin chuckled and shifted Ronnie in his arms. "I still can't believe it took me so long to realize you and Noah were a thing. The way you two look at each other makes it kinda obvious."

"You were sleep deprived from a newborn." Griff patted Justin's back and gave him a guilty look. "I'm sorry I didn't tell you when I figured it out."

Justin gave them both a knowing look. "It's okay. You've agreed not to keep anything from me again. You will tell me all your secrets, or I'll make Tanner give you both parking tickets."

Griff arched a brow. "Would he actually do it? I've never met a more strait-laced person in my life."

"He'd do it for Justin." Zed turned away from the mirror and pulled both of his brothers into his arms. "Thank you for being here, guys. I love you two so much and am proud to have you by my side." He looked over at the couch where Seth napped. "I'd say the same to Seth, but *teenagers.*"

"It's like all they do is eat, sleep, and have hormonal fueled breakdowns." Justin shook his head and shuddered. "I don't miss those years."

Griff snickered. "Me neither." He went and poked Seth. "Hey! Wake up. It's almost time to start."

Seth jerked awake and looked around. "Huh? Oh, yeah. The wedding." He grinned sleepily at Zed. "You look really good all fancied up."

A burst of happiness shot through him. "I love you guys."

"Ahh, we love you too, big guy." Justin hugged him. "Now, seriously, we need to get moving."

He followed his brothers from the tack room they'd made into a changing room for the wedding. They had decided to have the wedding at the ranch, since that was Noah's favorite place in the world. It also allowed the sandwich club to come to the wedding.

Gramps leaned against a post with Mary. "About time. Are you all ready to do this?"

Zed nodded. "Yes, sir."

Gramps pulled him into a hug. "None of that *sir* business. We're family, son. Let's get you married."

Mary danced in a circle and held up her flower basket. "I go first."

She had chosen leggings, a tutu, and suspenders for

her wedding outfit. Zed loved that she had insisted on miniature cowboy boots and one of Noah's old hats to complete her outfit. If she could, Mary would live in Noah's pocket.

"Thanks, Mary." Zed bent down and hugged her. "Love you, sweetheart."

Her arms tightened around him and she squeezed him as hard as she could. "Love you too." She looked up, eyes watering. "Mama and Daddy never said that a lot."

Seth winced and ran his hands over the blue ribbons braided through her blond hair. "Zed and Noah are different. It's okay to say how you feel with them. They listen."

Mary wiped her eyes. "They do. 'Kay, I'm ready."

They had decided against a wedding march song, and the ceremony would be held in the clearing between the two barns. Zed and his group were in one and Noah and his in the other. They planned to meet in the middle. He smiled thinking about it.

He leaned out the door and watched as Mary skipped down the path toward where their friends and family gathered. Olive was skipping her way from the other barn and tossing flowers all over the place. Noah's niece had chosen to wear a very poofy blue dress and black cat ears. The two girls met in the middle and grabbed hands before moving to the seat next to Tanner.

Justin's husband had Pike and Ronnie in his lap and Bea and Elijah's twins in the seats between him and

Grammy. The poor man already looked overwhelmed with all the kids.

Zed's eyes strayed to the back and he grinned. He could see Carrot and the miniatures at the back of the crowd of people with Saul and Emmet. The sandwich club was all *fancied up* as Seth would say with ribbons and flowers braided in their manes and tails.

"Abel, you're next," Gramps said, patting his grandson on the back.

Zed's friend patted his arm and winked as he left the barn and headed toward the center. Juan walked from Noah's side.

Slowly, Gramps cued Janelle, Seth, Justin, and Griff to leave the barn while Ray, Carter, Ernie, and Elijah met them in the clearing.

Zed snorted a laugh as Griff and Elijah waddled in from opposite sides and joined arms. "I love them. Is it bad that I really hope they give birth on the same day?"

Gramps shuddered. "Don't say things like that, son. It scares me just thinking about it."

Zed shifted and looked at Gramps. "You remember me saying that I was afraid of being like my dad?"

Gramps nodded, eyes soft. "I remember."

"I'm not like him." Zed shook his head. "I will never willingly leave Noah or my brothers and sister. If Noah and I decide to have kids, I'll never abandon them either. I'm in this forever."

Gramps patted his cheek. "I know. I'm glad you do too." He waved toward the clearing. "Shall we?"

Zed nodded and linked arms with the older man. Marco had insisted on walking Noah down the aisle, so

Gramps had stepped in and said he'd be doing the same for Zed. It felt odd, but nice too.

As they walked closer, Zed could see Noah in his matching suit. Zed didn't notice Captain Hoof in his own suit at first. The goat pranced at Noah's side, but Zed was too busy ogling his soon to be husband. Zed almost tripped a couple of times, but fortunately Gramps held him up.

Gramps chuckled and patted his hand. "Here you are, son. Safe and sound. Maybe keep your eyes in your head, huh?"

Zed flushed and cleared his throat. "Thanks, Gramps."

Marco and Gramps took their seats, and Zed tried to focus on something besides the freckles on Noah's nose and his gorgeous gap-toothed smile.

Noah gave him a heated look and leaned forward. "You look hot," he whisper-yelled.

Chuckles sounded from behind them.

Zed ignored them and grinned. "You look very handsome," he signed and wiggled his brows.

A tugging on his leg made him look down. "Damn it, Captain Hoof, don't eat my pants. Why couldn't you stay at the house like Tuffy?"

Their stupid goat just bleated at him and continued to munch on Zed's dress pants.

The minister cleared his throat and arched a brow. "May I?"

Noah snickered and nodded while Zed tried to shake the goat from his leg. Eventually he sighed and gave up. He didn't really need to keep these pants anyway.

Diane laughed at him from where she stood next to the minister. Noah's friend would sign the ceremony for Noah, so he didn't have to work to understand this special moment.

Zed shook his leg again. Nope, Captain Hoof was still chewing.

Zed soon forgot the goat as he watched Noah during the ceremony. He knew he'd never forget Noah's rapt face as he watched Diane sign or the feel of his love's warm hand in his. His family and friends stood at his back and his future was at his side.

NOAH KISSED PIKE'S CHUBBY CHEEK AND HUGGED HIM. "Make sure you poop as much as possible for Uncle Carter and Uncle Elijah, alright baby boy?"

Pike gurgled and pressed a wet kiss to Noah's cheek.

Noah reluctantly handed him to Carter and ignored his brother-in-law's glare. "Hey, I changed enough diapers for the twins. You owe me."

Mary hugged him around the waist, and Noah suspected she may be crying. He knelt in front of her. *Yep, those are tears.* "It's only one night, right?" She asked, eyes full of worry.

"Just one night." He hugged her close. He hadn't expected it would be so hard to leave the kids for the evening, even if it was for a very brief honeymoon night at Reuben and Ernie's cabin. "Go get another piece of cake and make sure you and Olive stay up as late as you want tonight."

Carter smacked his shoulder, making Noah and Mary laugh.

"I love you," she signed.

"I love you too, sweetheart." He kissed the top of her head, then let Olive pull her to the dance floor.

His niece gave him a wink and signed *I love you* over her shoulder.

He stood up and stared at Seth, arms raised.

The teenager rolled his eyes, but quickly moved into his hug. Noah squeezed him and shook him around, lifting him off his feet, before setting him back down. "I love you too, kid. Have fun at Jake's house, but not too much fun."

Seth shook as he laughed.

A few moments later, Noah and Zed drove away from the crowded reception. Noah closed his eyes and leaned back against the seat. *So many people.* He opened his eyes and looked at Zed's profile. His husband looked happy.

Noah's eyes caught on his own reflection in the side mirror. He barely recognized the look on his face. His eyes were soft with emotion and his lips swollen from the kisses Zed had stolen before they left the reception. *That's what happy looks like.*

It didn't take them long to arrive at the cabin. Noah smiled when he saw the flower arrangements and decorations covering the small front porch.

Zed stopped to study them, before turning back to

him and signing. "We need to take these home with us and plant them. Janelle made sure all they were all living arrangements."

Noah rolled his eyes, fighting a smile. "Of course, she did."

Janelle and Zed together were impossible. Plants had taken over his house, yard, and even encroached on the barns.

Noah tugged Zed into the house and straight to the bedroom. Three kids meant very little privacy and Noah was ready to celebrate.

He froze when he saw the bedroom. The bed was made and flower petals circled it. The air was scented with vanilla and some flower. *I feel like Zoe or Aunt Anna was here.*

Zed pulled him into his arms and bent to kiss him. Noah was effectively lost in the alpha's kiss and any romantic decorations were forgotten. They tugged at their clothes, somehow managing to undress without breaking their kiss.

Noah pushed Zed on the bed and straddled his legs. He wrapped his fingers around Zed's hard length and pumped, enjoying the silken heat in his hands.

Zed groaned and leaned up, cupping Noah's face and deepening their kiss. Noah lost track of time, his mind and body focused on Zed. He stroked the other alpha's dick a few more times, then cupped Zed's balls in one hand, testing the weight against his palm.

His hand slipped farther down, and he ran a finger over Zed's hole. He rubbed it for a moment before dipping the tip of one finger inside him.

Zed pulled back from their kiss, panting. "Fuck, Noah. I need you."

Noah's laugh felt rough. "Not as much as I need you." He kissed him again, deep and hard. "I swear I'm addicted to your damn kisses."

Noah pushed Zed back on the bed and stretched out alongside him. He ran his hands over Zed's chest and across his muscled stomach. His Marine's obsession with burpees paid off, and Noah certainly didn't mind.

Zed spread his legs and stroked his hard length, drawing Noah's attention. He moved down and took Zed's dick in his mouth, moaning at the taste of his husband's precum.

Zed cupped his head and pumped his hips, head falling back.

Noah savored the alpha's familiar smell and taste, wrapping his tongue around the tip of Zed's shaft and sucking. He slid Zed's dick as far down his throat as he could. When Noah felt Zed's body shuddering, he relaxed his throat and drank every drop of cum.

Zed's body went lax, so Noah grabbed the lube from the bedside table. He grinned at the red bow on the front. *Definitely Zoe.*

Noah turned back to his alpha and took his time stretching Zed's hole, teasing him with his fingers and tongue. By the time Noah pushed inside him, Zed was hard again.

Noah pumped his hips, moving slowly in and out of Zed's ass. He stroked Zed's dick as he moved inside him, angling his hips to hit his alpha's prostate as often as he could.

Zed's eyes rolled back in his head, and Noah knew he'd found the right spot. A few strokes later, Zed came again, splattering cum all over Noah's hand.

Noah licked his hand clean and let himself go, pounding into Zed's ass. A few moments later, he came hard. As soon as Zed's tight ass milked his dick of every last drop he had to give, Noah collapsed on top of him, panting hard.

Zed rolled them and pinned Noah beneath him. He stroked Noah's hair back from his face. "Thank you for loving me. I swear I will give you everything I have."

Noah leaned up and nipped Zed's chin. "You're my anchor, Z. I know exactly how lucky I am and plan to prove it to you every day for the rest of my life."

CHAPTER 18

*N*oah took his hat off and wiped his sweaty forehead as he watched Olive, her best friend Shelly, and Mary lead the miniatures around the freshly mowed hayfield. Jelly still had the light blue and grey ribbons in her mane from the wedding last week. Peanut and Butter had lost their own quickly.

Captain Hoof hopped around the horses, tail flitting back and forth and tags bouncing. Noah's goat made him smile, but he had to admit that Tuffy was the smart one. The cat napped on Butter's back and enjoyed the warm summer sun.

Carrot snuffled against his head, and Noah patted the gelding's neck. "Almost done, buddy."

The horse nuzzled his cheek one more time, then ran toward Stinkbug, who was currently rolling around on his back.

Seth tapped his arm and grinned. "Is this the last hayfield? I'm hungry."

"You're always hungry," Noah said, nudging him with his shoulder. "We'll get lunch after we finish here."

"Food," Seth signed. "Please."

Noah snorted a laugh and shoved him. "We literally have ten bales left to put on the truck."

Seth collapsed against him, eyes shimmering and his bottom lip trembling.

Noah hugged him and watched Jake and Emmet finish loading the bales while Dean and Saul tied them down. "Look, it's done, drama llama."

"I'll get these back to the ranch," Emmet signed, shaking his head as he laughed at Noah and Seth. He had been a huge help on the ranch the last couple of months and seemed a lot happier now that he was away from his brother. Noah didn't know their story, but he didn't like seeing Emmet upset, and his brother always seemed to set him off.

Saul stretched his arms over his head and laughed at something Dean said. Noah's other friend worked part-time on the ranch and full-time at the garage in Hobson Hills. Noah's cousin Shawn had been happy to hire another good mechanic.

Noah was just happy that two more friends were closer to him.

Mary ran toward him, her long blond braids flying behind her. "Noah," she signed. "Tuffy and me are hungry."

Seth gave him a look. "Tuffy's hungry, Noah. This is important."

Noah shoved him away with a laugh. "Should we go to the diner, the Irish Rose, or Honey Buns?" he asked

Mary, signing slowly so she could follow along. She had started to pick up more signs recently, so he tried to sign more with her at home.

"Pancakes for lunch," she said aloud, bouncing in place.

"The diner it is," he said with a smile. "Olive, Shelly, is that alright?"

"Pancakes are always alright, Uncle Noah." Olive hugged him tight, then grabbed Mary's hand and pulled her to the car.

Shelly gave him a shy look and nodded before following her friends.

"Jake, you're coming with us, right?" Seth asked, eyes hopeful.

Noah shared an amused look with Dean. The two teenagers had become almost inseparable over the past month since they'd both been working on the ranch during the summer.

"Can I, Papa?" Jake asked, eyes on Dean.

"Sure." Dean patted Noah's shoulder. "I'll drive these two, if you take the girls."

"Deal, but you have to bring Emmet and Saul too." Noah arched his back and winced. "You know how annoying they are on a drive."

Dean gave him a pitiful look. "I thought you liked me."

Noah laughed. "Only sometimes."

He hurried to top the water off in the trough next to the pasture's gate. Usually he just used this field for hay, but Captain Hoof and the horses looked too happy to move. Peanut stomped her feet when Jelly rolled around in the grass like Stinkbug. *Uh oh. There's dissention in the ranks.*

He must have lingered too long because Captain Hoof ran over and hopped around him.

"Sorry, buddy. You know Gib won't let you in the diner."

Mary ran to him, face flushed with happiness. "Come on, Dad. I'm hungry." As soon as the words left her, her eyes widened, and she covered her mouth.

He blinked, eyes watering. "Did you just call me dad?"

"I'm sorry," she said. She spoke too fast for him to understand the rest.

"Slow down, M."

"I'm sorry," she said again. "I love you, and it just slipped out."

Noah hugged her tightly, lifting her off her feet. "I love you too. It's okay if you call me dad or Noah, either one." Her stomach grumbled against him. "Your tummy is telling me it's time for lunch."

He set her down and noticed Olive watching him with a huge smile on her face. "You're a good dad," she signed.

He wiped his eyes. "Okay, let's go eat. Captain Hoof, you can come, but I'll have to leave you tied up all alone outside."

The goat ignored him and ran to Olive. Noah winced. The goat may have already learned that they would take their food to the park to eat.

~

LATER THAT NIGHT, NOAH STRADDLED ZED'S LAP AND kissed him again, mouths pressed hard together as their tongues dueled.

Zed's hands ran down Noah's naked back and cupped his ass, pulling their hips together. Noah moaned, enjoying the press of their bodies. He rocked slowly against Zed, wishing they hadn't worn pants to bed.

Zed reached between them, and Noah leaned back, letting his alpha free their erections. He panted when Zed pressed their dicks together and slowly began jacking them.

He curled a hand around Zed's neck and pulled him in for another heated kiss. He could never get enough of Zed's taste. He cried out against Zed's mouth when he came and felt the heat of his cum soak his stomach.

Zed's chest rumbled with his own groans, and he came soon after, soaking them both. Zed buried his face against Noah's neck and pressed his hand to Noah's chest in a very familiar sign. "I love you."

"I love you too." Noah stroked his hands over Zed's back, savoring the moment between them. Both of their jobs kept them busy in the summer, and they definitely had less privacy. Despite that, or maybe because of it, they'd grown closer and more reliant on one another the last two months.

Noah knew Zed was his in a way that no one else was, just like he filled a place in Zed that no one could. Elijah had spoken with him about how it felt to love Carter, but Noah hadn't gotten it. To him, love was family and security.

His love for Zed held hints of that too, but it was more. Zed was his person. He was his best friend, his lover, the man who adored him, but still challenged him. Zed accepted Noah just as he was and didn't demand anything from him except honesty. He let Noah be grumpy and tired when he needed to be and took care of him when Noah didn't feel like caring for himself. *My person.*

Zed leaned back and cupped Noah's face before reaching over to the nightstand to grab Noah's phone. It was vibrating, but Noah hadn't noticed. Whoever it was, they were calling instead of texting.

Zed raised a brow, and Noah nodded, yawning. He was more than happy to let Zed deal with it.

He slid off the bed and went to the bathroom to clean up and grabbed a fresh pair of pajama pants from the dresser. Mary had taken to grabbing Pike and bringing him in to wake them up early in the morning.

He paused when he noticed Zed sitting still on the bed. His alpha watched him with sad eyes. "What happened?"

"Your dad was killed late last night," Zed signed. His hands hung in the air, and he looked torn. "I'm so sorry, love."

Noah looked away, eyes focusing on the window shelf of potted succulents to his left. His stomach twisted, but he honestly couldn't say what he felt. *Dad's dead,* he thought, trying to make himself react. *He fucked up and got killed. He's gone. There's no redemption for our relationship. He'll never be a real grandfather or father. He's dead.*

He didn't move when Zed pulled him into his arms. Noah pressed his face into Zed's shoulder and tried to cry. Tried to feel. *Nothing.*

Noah held Elijah's hand as they watched them lower their dad's casket into the ground. It was a beautiful summer day, and Noah wanted to be anywhere but there. Steven Wilson would be buried with generations of other Wilsons, but whether or not his family would mourn him was another question.

Marco, Anna, and Barry were hard-faced and angry. Steven hadn't been a particularly likable person, little less a good brother. All of their kids, Noah and Elijah's cousins, were there to show their respect too, but like their parents, they hadn't liked the man. They were there for Noah, Elijah, Gramps, and Grammy.

Noah's grandparents had taken Steven's death hard. He thought maybe, like him, they had held out hope that Steven would suddenly become a decent son and father.

Mary's small hand on his back and Seth's hand on his shoulder were a reassurance. Pike and the rest of the Wilson littles were with a sitter, but his two eldest had insisted on being with him.

Juan stood next to the minister and signed for Noah. The minister spoke of living life to the fullest, loving one's family, and taking no regrets to the grave. It wasn't exactly reflective of how they felt about

Noah's dad, but he supposed the ceremony wasn't for the dead. It was for the living.

Noah laced the fingers of his free hand with Zed's. His husband had held him last night when he'd finally broken apart. He'd let him ramble on about nothing and did his best to soothe Noah. He'd held him again when he woke up screaming from a nightmare.

Zed knew how he felt. He'd gone through the same thing with his own dad's death a few months ago. Noah remembered what Zed had said the first time they had met. *Parents have a way of fucking with our heads.*

Noah took a breath and let it out slowly. Steven Wilson was dead, and Noah needed to let the past die with him. He had one hell of a future to look forward to.

Noah gently rocked his newborn niece, Ellie, while Zed paced the front porch with Griff's newborn, Rose. Ellie's little poof of black hair stood straight up on her head, and her little round cheeks were baby soft. He couldn't stop rubbing them.

The whole Wilson family and all their friends were gathered at Gramps and Grammy's home for Noah's grandparents' anniversary party. Mary and the other Wilson littles ran around the house while everyone ate delicious food and visited with one another. Seth played soccer in the front yard with the other teenagers, and Pike was currently in the napping room with a few other babies.

Noah's eyes went to Elijah and Carter. The two were snuggled on a bench nearby. The way they looked at each other didn't spark envy in Noah's chest anymore.

Zed settled beside him on the front steps and patted

his knee. The alpha's crooked smile sent heat straight to Noah's gut.

He knew his own face probably looked as embarrassingly mushy as his brother's. *I've found my forever.*

Charybdis Station Chronicles – science fiction/fantasy, mpreg

The Blue Solace Series

http://mybook.to/BlueSolaceSeries

1. The Mercenary's Mate
2. The General's Mate
3. The Soldier's Mate
4. The Lieutenant's Mate
5. The Engineer's Mate
6. The Captain's Mate
7. The Rebel's Mate

Charybdis Station

1. Death's Mate – *Coming Soon*
2. Fire's Mate – *Coming Soon*
3. Rune and Silas – *Coming Soon*

The Hobson Hills Omegas – non-shifter, mpreg, omegaverse

http://mybook.to/HHOseries

1. Falling for the Omega
2. Snow Kisses for My Omega
3. Romancing the Omega

4. Healing the Omega
5. A Pint for my Omega
6. Unraveling the Omega
7. The Alpha's Christmas Wish
8. Convincing the Alpha
9. Title TBA – Sheriff McKenzie's Book – *Coming Soon*

Hobson Hills Shorts – short stories from the world of Hobson Hills Omegas

1. The Beta's Love Song – http://mybook.to/BetaLoveSong
2. Bennett's Dream – http://mybook.to/BennettsDream
3. Justin's Journey – http://mybook.to/JustinJourney
4. Grey's Gift – http://mybook.to/GreyGift
5. Hobson Hills Shorts: Volume One – http://mybook.to/HHOShortsVolumeOne

Holiday Omegas Shorts – holiday short stories from the world of The Silver Isles – paranormal, mpreg

http://mybook.to/HolidayOmegaSeries

1. Cauldron Cake Pops and a Witch's Kiss
2. Sugar Cookies and a Witch's Love
3. Candy Hearts and a Witch's Ring
4. Carrot Cake and a Witch's Surprise – *Coming in June, 2020*

The Silver Isles – paranormal, mermen, mpreg

http://mybook.to/TheSilverIsles

1. The Guppy Prince
2. The Not so Little Merman
3. The Sea Witch – *Coming Soon*

If you would like to keep up with releases, please like and follow me on Instagram (@c.w._gray) or Facebook (@cwgrayauthor), join C.W. Gray's Reading Nook on Facebook, or visit my website at https://cwgray-author.com.

Unedited excerpt from *The Mercenary's Mate* – Book One in the Blue Solace Series

Silverlight System, Planet Vextonar

"Next up is a real gem, gentle folks!" The auctioneer leered toward the large crowd at the bottom of the stage. He was a Betonize-human hybrid, sharp teeth a glaring white. "This little girl's part Prime and part Lower. Don't see that on Vextonar too often."

The crowd's boisterous laughter and cheering filled the room. Eight people had already been auctioned off, and the day was still young. Leti Ando gritted his teeth and awkwardly shuffled his feet. The bulky cast on his lower leg made him slower than normal, and there were too many strangers here, too much movement. He wanted to be in his rooms, reading the new Old-Earth journal he'd gotten his hands on.

Draif shot him a sympathetic look. Leti's best friend

was no less uncomfortable in the auction house but had insisted on coming with him. "You knew it'd be like this, Master," Draif whispered.

Leti glared at his friend, his black eye and busted lip protesting the expression. "I hate it when you call me that."

Draif gave him a small smile, dark eyes on the stage. "I know. Why do you think I do it?" His smile faded. "It's her, Leti."

Leti startled, stumbling and knocking into some of the men around him. He did his best to ignore the grumbles, his heart beating fast in his chest. Monty slipped from his head to his shoulder, and Draif grabbed his arm to steady him. For such a small, slender man, Draif had a strong and sure grip that came in handy when Leti's clumsiness attacked.

Leti ignored the grumbles around him, eyes locked on the stage. A modestly dressed woman stood tall. She held a whimpering, blanket-wrapped bundle in her arms.

"This little lady is up for sale," the Auctioneer said. "She comes from a Prime daddy and his mistress, a Lower woman. Unnamed infant, but good potential. Mommy's dead and Daddy don't want a Lower brat, so there won't be no contest of ownership once she's bought. We'll start bidding at 250? Can I get 250?"

Leti sighed and closed his eyes. "I can't believe Father is selling his own child. I hate that he deals in slavery at all, but his own daughter?"

"Yeah, well, he didn't seem to like your opinion too much last night when you brought it up." Draif grabbed his hand and squeezed. "Not that he needs much excuse to beat the shit out of you. It was the threat to sell you too that worries me the most."

It wasn't appropriate for a bed-slave to hold his master's hand, but the two of them had never been *appropriate*. Nothing was normal about a Prime citizen who didn't have sex with his bed-slave, little less treat him like a slave, and nothing was normal about a bed-slave who was demisexual and had a scarred face and damn good fighting skills.

Draif had been Leti's best friend since they were both fifteen. Leti's father gave him to his son and told him to dominate the "broken" slave and prove himself a man. The arrogant Prime often told his son that he was so fat and awkward that no one would ever want him, especially with his attention always on his studies and research.

Leti might be a breeder male, able to have children, but his father assured him no one would ever offer for him like they would a daughter. And love? According to his father, no one could ever love him, not even some mixed breed alien. Being a breeder male showed his blood was too diluted to be human enough. There was too much Wello blood in his ancestry. Father always blamed Leti's mother for it, but never to her face. He was an arrogant bully, not stupid.

In his father's mind, a bed-slave would guarantee that Leti would at least be a man in the bedroom. Leti tried not to complain too much, though. Draif had proven to be the best thing that ever happened to him. He was his loyal confidant and best friend from the start and soon became his assistant, body guard, and overall jack-of-all-trades.

Where Leti struggled in anything outside of his books and pets, Draif could seemingly master any skill if he set his mind to it. More importantly, though, Leti loved Draif more than anything in all the galaxies. He was his brother in all but blood. His family.

"620 to the Drall in the corner. Can I get 630, anyone? 630?"

"Is your lawyer bidding?" Draif whispered.

Leti looked at his communicator. "Yes. He'll keep topping whatever's offered. She'll be ours in a few minutes."

"You father won't like that, Leti. What are we going to do? We can't hide her in your rooms until she's eighteen. I guess we could put her in Wobble's stable, but who wants to live with an Old-Earth Llama?" Draif paused and eyed his friend. "Well, except for you."

Leti grinned. "When I get her, you are going to take her to the spaceport. Talk with Dottie. She's going to sneak all of us on a random ship going out of the system. Father would be alerted if we used our passports, so we have to sneak, at least at first. Once we're out of the Silverlight system, I can tear up your contract as well as hers. You'll both be free."

Draif squeezed his hand tight. His eyes left the stage, widened in disbelief. "We're leaving the system?"

Leti snorted. "I've given you several chances to leave over the last ten years, but you wouldn't go."

"I couldn't possibly leave you behind. I love you," he said with no hesitancy. "What about your menagerie?"

Draif looked at the vexal newt happily perched on Leti's shoulder. "Monty here wouldn't be a problem, but you can't possibly expect to sneak all of them onboard a ship and I know you won't leave them." Draif shook his head, dumbfounded. "What about money? How will you survive? I can easily get work, but you're a trained historian. They aren't exactly rolling in credits." He paused, already forming a plan. "I could work and you could stay home and take care of the baby. You'd be good at that. You love. It's your thing, and in the end, that's all it really takes. We can figure out how to feed her and change a diaper."

"1050! Can I get 1100? Anyone? 1100?"

"Dottie assures me it will be fine. She's picked out a Drellian cargo vessel and my pets are heading there as we speak, even Wobble." Leti checked his comm, then continued, "As for money, I've been saving for a long time. Do you really think I spend all the credits Father gives me monthly?"

"He's always complaining that you drain his pocket, but I thought he was just being cheap. All you buy are books on your tablet, presents for me, and things for the pets. I think the most expensive thing you bought was the tablet. It came from the Anchor's Rest System, right? Our system is seriously behind on tech."

Leti nodded. "I don't usually use more than a quarter of the allowance. I've been saving my pay from my publications too. It's certainly not much, but I didn't become a historian to make money. I never thought I'd have to." Leti laughed ruefully. "I'm a privileged Prime, right?"

Draif let go of his hand and smacked his arm. "No self-deprecation allowed! We are who we are, there's no changing that. Especially on this world. It's not like you can change castes and become a Worker. Anyways, the gods know that no one deserves to be related to your father or psycho mother." He smiled sadly and nodded toward Leti's broken ankle. "Their love hurts."

Draif looked worried. "Are you going to pack and bring my things too?"

"Of course! Melinda has already started packing for us."

"Will she alert your father?"

Leti checked his comm again. Things were on track. "No. She's the one who urged me to start saving credits when I was twelve. Once we leave, she's going to go to Rothwell and work with her daughter."

"Good." Draif's couldn't seem to stop smiling. "We're really doing this?"

"1520 to the gentleman at the front! 1600 anyone? 1600? Going once. Going twice. Sold to the gentleman in the blue coat!"

Despite his worry, Leti grinned. "Yes. We're really doing this."

Buy Here: My Book

Excerpt from *The Guppy Prince*, book one in The Silver Isles.

Dover Rees floated in the deepest part of his creek, enjoying the rushing sound of the waterfall to his right. Sunlight filtered through the water, glinting off the deep blue of his guppy tail. His thin and delicate caudal fin spread out like an elegant fan, dancing through the warm water as he swayed.

His favorite smooth and colorful pebbles were strewn around below him, and he admired the shells he had collected and placed beside them. Dover breathed deeply and enjoyed the peace and quiet. No one mocked him or bossed him around. No one watched him with cold eyes and hidden smirks. *I wish I could stay here forever.*

Sudden movement beside him jarred him from his thoughts and he laughed when Chubber grabbed a bright pink stone in his small brown paws and swam away. Dover's otter friend liked to steal Dover's shinies then share them with him again later.

A brook trout swam past him and Dover debated grabbing it for an early lunch, but he wasn't too hungry yet. Lately, he'd been eating less and less, and he couldn't make himself care.

The quiet water around him hummed as Nami quickly swam to him. His best friend's guppy tail was a lovely pink pattern with black dots, and her short black hair floated around her head. The cat with a mermaid tail on her black tankini top made him smile. He loved her purr-maid shirts.

"Have you eaten today, Your Highness?" she asked.

Dover scowled. "Don't call me that."

"When you're acting like a pouting asswipe, that's what you get called." Nami wrapped her arms around him and settled her head on his shoulder. "What's wrong with you, Dover?"

Dover had no answer for her. All he knew was he felt empty inside and it was harder and harder to get up in the morning. "I think I ate some bad clams."

"Every day for the past two months?" Nami leaned back and glared at him, her dark eyes seeing right through him.

Chubber came to his rescue, swimming in between them and wrapping his lean body across Dover's shoulders. "Chubber wants to get a snack."

Nami sighed, bubbles filling the water around her. "Mom is in your cottage making lunch. You're worrying us, bluetail."

Dover stroked a hand through her hair, then shoved

her down and pushed up, swimming toward the surface.

"Damn it!" Nami swam after him.

He laughed, heart warming. *Someone cares about me.* It wasn't his family, but Nami and her mom were closer to him than his parents or any of his twelve siblings.

Chubber clung to his back and nibbled on his ear until he mentally apologized. Chubber cared about him the most.

His creek was deep, but it didn't take him long to reach the surface. Shauna waited for them on the shore, hands on her hips. Chubber's mother, Shell, stood on her hind legs beside the mermaid, chirping loudly. Uh oh. He really was in trouble.

"You didn't eat breakfast, did you?" The wind blew strands of Shauna's pink hair across her face, ruining her glare.

"Sorry, Shauna."

She sighed. "I made your favorite."

"Grilled shrimp salad?" Dover's stomach rumbled.

"With avocado, papaya, mango, and pineapple. All your favorites." Shauna gave him a soft look. "Come eat, bluetail."

Dover summoned his human legs and a few seconds later, walked out of the creek, naked, with Chubber clinging to his shoulder. Shauna handed him a deep teal sarong, and he tied it about his waist.

Shell crawled up his leg and into his arms, then rubbed her slick furry face against his. She was a bit heavier than Chubber, but he was still a baby.

"Why does he get all the loving?" Nami asked, grumbling as she tied a sarong around her own waist.

Dover chuckled when Shauna arched an eyebrow at her daughter. "Did you say something, sweetness?"

"No, ma'am," Nami said, wincing.

"You two come eat lunch." Shauna turned around and walked toward Dover's large cottage.

Dover closed his eyes for a moment and savored the feel of the moss-covered rocks under his feet, and the comfortable breeze quickly drying his curly blue hair. He loved his home so much. It was his sanctuary.

Buy Here: https://amzn.to/2q9Q8en